UNEXPECTED STORMS

THE UNEXPECTED SERIES, BOOK 4

STACY EATON

CHAPTER ONE

HARVEY

"Hey, man!" I stepped through the front door at Maggie Valor's house and clapped hands and shoulders with Greg Blaire, a friend and co-worker at Safety Zone Security. "It's about time you came back to the real world!"

"No doubt," he said as he let me go and shut the door behind me. "Come on in; everyone is out back."

"How does it feel returning after a five-week exile?" I asked him. Maggie and Greg had been off the grid that long after they had been held hostage during a botched robbery—that Maggie herself had screwed up without knowing. After the event, a few of the hostages had turned up dead, and someone had come after Maggie, but luckily Greg had been there and took the guy down.

It wasn't the guys involved with the robbery and kidnapping that had been worrisome; it was the cartel that those guys had been working for. They hadn't wanted to be given up by Chuck and Len, so they silenced them and several other witnesses too. The police had asked anyone who was left to head out of town.

A couple of weeks ago, a few of the witnesses came back, not Maggie or Greg, but a few others, and so far, there hadn't been any threats and no further signs that the cartel wanted any other retribution. Hence the reason Maggie and Greg finally came out of hiding.

"It feels great, and it sure is nice to be back at home."

"Home?" I glanced around. "This is home now? Are things going that well for you and Maggie?" When the two of them had gone into lockdown, Greg had been trying everything he could to keep distance between himself and his former high school sweetheart.

Greg frowned at me. "You know what I mean, Harv, home as in back here."

"So, you and Maggie aren't living together now?"

"I didn't say that." He chuckled and slapped my back. "Go get yourself a drink. I have to grab something from the kitchen."

"Alright, I'll see you out there." On the back deck, Alex and his pregnant wife, Lexi, were seated on a gliding love seat, and Trevor had his infant son, Devon, on his lap, while his fiancée, Davina, helped Maggie with something at the food table. Alice was over there too, along with Mike and two pretty women that I didn't know. Mike was laughing at something that one of the women had said.

Standing off to the side, talking shit to one another was Jake, our boss, along with Drake, Wyatt, Joe, and Brett, who were all part-timers with our company. I made the rounds, saying hello to everyone, and Greg tossed me a beer as he came back out of the house.

A few minutes later, Greg had his arm around Maggie when he called us all to attention. "Thanks to all of you for coming. While Maggie and I had a great time being on vacation for a full five weeks, we are very happy to be home and to have you all here."

"You guys married yet?" Jake called out with a laugh.

"No, we are not, and we aren't in any rush to do that either." Maggie didn't look the least bit upset by his words as she smiled up at him. "But we did reconnect nicely after nineteen years, and I know I feel like I know her better than I ever did. I'm pretty sure she knows every single one of my bad habits now, and she is still willing to stand here beside me."

Brett whistled loudly as Wyatt joked, "Damn, anyone who can put up with his shit, and I mean that literally, is good in my book."

Laughter and a few crude jokes about bathroom etiquette went around the group for a few moments.

Maggie was laughing, a huge smile on her face. "Do you know how many times I got yelled at for putting the toilet paper on wrong?"

"Wait!" Trevor snapped as he threw up his hand. "Don't tell me that you put it on so that it hangs under?"

"Of course I do, doesn't everybody?" Maggie replied with a serious face.

"No way!" Jake called out loudly. "Even the patent office has it on record that it has to hang over!"

"But that's crap!" Lexi joined the conversation. "Just because when they did a drawing of toilet paper, they had it hanging over, that doesn't mean that is the end-all way to do it."

Alex barked out a laugh and pointed at Lexi. "But that's how you hang it!"

She shrugged. "I know, but that doesn't mean there is a right or wrong way to do it."

The debate continued for a few more minutes before Greg put his hands up to get everyone's attention. "Alright, we can finish the great toilet paper debate later. There is something that Maggie and I wanted to share with you."

"Well, if you aren't getting married, are you having a baby?" Davina asked. Maggie and Greg looked at one another and held each other a little tighter as Greg shook his head.

"No, no babies in our future," he said with a bright smile.

"What we wanted to share with you is that Maggie is now the newest official employee at SZS, as our official media liaison!"

"Oh, that's great!" Lexi clapped excitedly and Jake approached them, giving Maggie a hug.

"She's actually been working for us already," Jake said. "When I got back from our medical supply delivery, I shared with her a bunch of photographs and videos that I took. She's been working on some social media advertising, and if I'm not mistaken, just sold our story to a prominent Washington D.C. paper."

"I sure did," Maggie said brightly.

Alice asked Jake, "Maggie is the one that made that video you showed me the other day?"

"Yep."

Alice turned wide bright eyes toward Maggie. "It was fantastic! I hope he paid you extra for that, because you even managed to make Jake look like a decent human being."

Everyone howled in laughter. "You're funny, Alice," Jake muttered toward her, and the two of them stared at one another for a moment. Were they sleeping together? If they weren't, they should be because the amount of sexual tension that radiated off of them was almost mind-blowing.

"No, he didn't pay me extra, Alice, but I'll keep that in mind the next time he wants me to change something out to make him look better."

"What a narcissist," Trevor joked.

"Maggie has also been working with Mike on a new website design, and on Monday, we are going to roll it out, so make sure you all take a good look at it. If things go as well as we anticipate, we are hoping to bring the rest of you PTers on full time."

Drake put his beer in the air. "Hear, hear! I'm ready."

"We have some other things in the works, too, and on Monday we need to meet as a group and go over some upcoming changes," Jake continued.

"Hey, did you forget that I'm on vacation this week?" I called out.

Jake turned to me. "And if I'm not mistaken, you aren't going anywhere or doing anything. You took the time off to burn."

"Yeah, so. Coming into the office for a meeting kind of defeats the purpose."

"Well, you could not come and then find out about all of it next week when you return."

I rolled my eyes at him. "What time on Monday?"

"One, and since it is going to be all of us, let's meet at the training facility. Actually, let's make it noon, and Alice can order us lunch, and we can eat while we talk about the new website and show you some of the videos that Maggie has put together."

"I'm the lunch girl now?" Alice barked, and her dark-brown eyes slit closed as she glared at him. She was almost as headstrong and volatile as our boss, and I knew she hated when he volunteered her for things that were not in her job description.

"I got it, Alice," Maggie said with a wink to Alice.

Jake shook his head and muttered something under his breath.

Greg announced after that they were putting the food on the grill, and we all milled around talking and snacking on finger foods while the cooking got underway with Greg and Jake.

My cellphone vibrated in my pocket of my shorts, and I pulled it out to see my sister, Holly, was calling. I stepped away from the group of people I was speaking with and answered, "Hey, Holly, what's up?"

"Harv, I need your help." She sounded close to panic, and she never sounded like that. My sister was normally calm as a cucumber.

"Are you alright?"

"Yes, I'm alright, but I need your help."

"Anything you need."

My sister was five years younger than me and one of my best

friends. When I'd gone into the military, leaving her had been the hardest thing I had to do. Especially as she had been just starting high school and getting involved with boys.

When I got out of the Marines three years ago after a shoulder injury, Holly and I had clicked right back into hanging out together. Except now instead of movie night and popcorn, we had dinner dates and drinks.

"Really? Anything?" she asked, and I heard the uncertainty in her voice.

"Of course, Holly. Whatever you need. I'm there for you."

"Oh, my god, Harv! You have no idea how much that means to me! Seriously, I was freaking out, but this is going to work!"

I chuckled. "Okay, what did I just volunteer for?"

"I'll explain it all on Monday. You're still off this week, right?"

"Yeah, but I need to attend a meeting Monday afternoon, why?"

"We can work around that," she said and sounded excited.

"Alright, but again, what did I volunteer for?"

"It's a surprise, but I know you will love it! It's going to be so awesome."

"You're lucky that I love you, kid."

She laughed. "Harv, I'm thirty-five years old now; I think you can stop calling me kid."

"Nope, you will always be a kid to me."

"You are hopeless. Okay, I'll text you the address of where to meet me, and wear something comfortable."

"Comfortable? What are you going to have me doing? Moving stuff? Oh, god! You're going to make me paint, aren't you?"

She laughed. "No, nothing like that. Well, you'll be moving around a lot, but you won't be painting. Just wear comfortable clothes."

"Alright, fine."

"Love you, Harv! I appreciate this so much! I'll talk to you later."

"I'll see you on Monday," I told Holly before I hung up and returned to the group I'd been talking to.

"Problem?" Wyatt asked.

"Nah, my sister needs my help with something."

"I didn't know you had a sister," Joe said.

"Oh, yeah," Drake said, "she is one fine woman."

"Hey, you watch it," I growled at him. "That is my sister you are talking about."

"Who is a grown woman and does not need you to hover over her," Drake added.

"I only hover over her because the last two men she was with did a number on her. I'm not going to let that happen again."

"You should bring her around sometime," Joe said.

I frowned at him. "Yeah, why? So that you can drool and hound dog all over her? I don't think so. I just told you that I'm not going to let another guy take advantage of her, and you immediately say you want to meet her." I laughed. "You are not her type, Joe."

"Man, you have no idea how well I treat girls."

Drake busted out a laugh. "Yeah, well, maybe you'll be ready for a serious relationship with an adult woman when you stop referring to them as girls or chicks."

"I didn't call his sister a chick," Joe said quickly.

Wyatt laughed. "No, not her and not today, but you do use that term quite often."

"I'm talking about baby chickens." Joe grinned.

I shoved his arm. "Bullshit! Dude, this is why I'm not going to allow my sister to get around you. She is totally out of your league."

Drake smiled. "I have to agree with you, Melton, your sister is way above his level."

"Oh, and you think she is closer to yours?" Joe joked back.

"I didn't say that, but yeah, I'm pretty sure I'm closer to her normal standards than you are."

I held my hand up. "You all can stop right now. There is no way that Holly would date any of you meatheads. She's into artsy guys."

"Hey, I enjoy the arts," Brett said.

"Body paints are not the arts," Drake said with a laugh.

"I beg to differ," Joe tacked on, and our conversation veered off of my sister, thankfully, and onto other subjects.

I didn't think about my sister's request to meet her again until Sunday night when she texted me an address and reminded me to wear something comfortable.

Are you going to tell me what I'm going to be doing?

You're going to be helping me, and someone else out, and you're going to have fun while you do it.

Someone else? An uneasy feeling slipped down my spine, and I had a feeling that I was not going to have fun with whatever my sister was roping me into.

CHAPTER TWO

ALI

"*I* don't think I can do this," I said to my best friend Charlie. "Why did I let you talk me into this?"

Charlie gave me her best what-the-hell look that she could muster. "I didn't talk you into this! You suggested it, Ali! I told you when you first came to me with the idea that I didn't think it was a good one."

I frowned at her as I jerked back. "But why isn't it a good idea?"

Charlie laughed, not just a funny tee-hee, but a full-on throw-the-head-back-and-cackle kind of laugh. "Because you are talking about a blind date, Ali. You—who doesn't even date—is going to go on, not one or two, but three blind dates, and you aren't even going to talk to them. You're going to dance with them—dance. It makes no sense, Ali, even for you."

"But don't you see, this will be the best! I don't have to come up with small talk; I just dance with them, and then if I enjoy it, and I like them, then I can dance again."

"How do you know if you will like them? You think fancy footwork is going to help you decide that a guy is worth getting to know?"

"No, it's about chemistry. It's about locking eyes and seeing if you can trust someone without them even opening their mouth. It's about having fun and being different. Geez, Charlie, you've been on those dating apps for months. What has it gotten you?"

She shrugged as she sipped from her iced tea glass. "I'm not saying it's wrong. I'm saying that it's weird, and it's absurdly weird for you."

"Weird? I love to dance, and I'm thirty-four years old. It's been four years since I was in a serious relationship, and I can feel my eggs drying up as we sit here."

Charlie winced. "That's gross to think about."

"It's the truth. I'm not getting any younger, and I want a man in my life. I want a family, and I want to plan a future."

"How about some fries with that?" she added drolly.

"Come on, Charlie, I'm serious here."

"Serious about what?"

"Finding love. I want to find love!"

"And you honestly think that you will find love by dancing with strangers? You don't even like to take an Uber because the driver is a stranger."

"It's not the same thing. These men are vetted. They go through criminal background checks and medical exams to make sure they are healthy enough to participate. They also have extensive interviews, and one of the people that conducts the interviews is a psychologist. The producer told me that they weed out quite a few people in that process because they have odd tastes, or just weird the interviewers out."

She gave me a dubious look. "Weird the interviewers out?"

I pursed my lips. "Come on, do you really think this is a bad idea?"

"For you? Yes. For anyone else? No, not at all."

I startled back slightly. "What do you mean, for me, yes?"

"Ali, I love you to death, you know that. We have been

besties since freshman year in college, but I can't see you doing this. I'm worried that you will freak out at the last minute and end up not doing it, and then you will be mortified and stress over it for weeks."

I opened my mouth to deny it, but closed it and wilted slightly in my seat. "Okay, I get what you are saying." I pushed some of my salad around on my plate. "But what if this works for me? What if I go out there and dance with these men and find one that I connect with? And what if I can do it without ever having to open my mouth and say anything? What if I have such a connection with one of them that it leads to a third date, a fourth, maybe a future?"

She blinked rapidly for a few seconds. "Do I need to remind you that you can't dance? You trip over your own feet walking from the room, Ali. How do you think that you are going to dance when you are so nervous that you'll probably puke? Five minutes ago, you were asking me why I talked you into doing this after you said *you* weren't sure you'd be able to do it. Now you are acting like you are trying to convince *me*."

"I'm not trying to convince you." I paused. "Okay, maybe I am trying to convince you so that I convince myself that it's a good idea."

She rubbed her temples like she had a headache coming on.

"Look, I want to do it. I do. I really, really do, and I need you on my side. I need you to encourage me because you are right. When it gets time to go out there, I might be so nervous that I forget everything, and I'll need someone to pick me up after I trip over my own feet and pass out from mortification."

She reached over the table and put her hand on my arm. "And I will be there, taking pictures the whole time."

I laughed. "No, you won't! There will be enough cameras there to capture my humiliation. Speaking of pictures, are you still working on your line for the gallery show?"

"Yep, I am."

For a few minutes, we talked about a couple of the new photos that Charlie had taken recently and the plans for her show. I loved her photographs, loved watching her work. Her pictures were conversation pieces, no matter who saw them. She was incredible, and not just with one subject, but with just about anything that she put into the frame of her lens. She could bring life to a wall, or humanness to a frog. Her talent was exceptional, and I envied her.

Not only was she an incredible photographer, but she was a wonderful person too. She went out of her way to help people, and she was my best friend to boot!

After lunch, we spent the afternoon browsing our favorite boutiques downtown, and we were coming out of one when my cellphone rang with a number that looked familiar, but I didn't recall immediately.

"Hello?"

"Ali? This is Holly Melton, the producer of *May I Have This Dance.*"

"Hi, Holly. How are you?"

"I'm great. I just wanted to check in with you and make sure that you are all set to get started tomorrow."

"I am. I'm looking forward to it." As I said the words, a mixture of panic and excitement whooshed through my veins.

"Oh, I'm so glad to hear that. I also wanted to let you know that there has been a slight change."

"Oh?"

"Yeah, one of your dates had to back out, he was in a water-skiing accident and broke his leg."

"Oh, no! Poor guy!"

"But don't worry, I had a backup just in case, and he's excited to step in."

"Alright, and you think he might be someone that I'll like?"

"Oh, Ali, I know this man personally. He will be perfect."

I chuckled a little uneasily. "Well, I'm leaving that up to you. I think I have enough to worry about."

She laughed. "That is for sure! Preparing for your dates is going to be intense."

"I do not doubt that," I replied with a snicker.

"You'll do great. I know you will. I'll see you on Monday."

"Thank you, Holly."

Charlie and I headed into another store, and as I browsed the racks, my mind was a million miles away. Was it possible to find love through dancing? Was I only kidding myself? Was I setting myself up to fail?

I didn't want to fail. I love to dance, and I know that I wasn't very good at it, but I did love to dance. I honestly felt like music and movement were a different form of communication, and since the natural way of finding someone wasn't working for me, maybe this one would. Perhaps I wouldn't find love, but maybe, just maybe, this could help me get out of my shell a little bit, and I could try to find it another way later if this didn't work.

Or possibly, one of my three dates would twirl me off my feet and carry me into the sunset. I frowned as I fingered a blouse on a hanger. When had I become such a hopeless romantic? Maybe I was spending too much time reading romance books, and not enough time searching through the reality of life. Not that I had much time to read these days, but it was more time than I spent socializing with other people.

It was so easy to get lost in a fictional world. A good author could suck you right into their words, and weave such a masterful tale that you never wanted to leave. It would be as if you were living those moments, feeling those emotions, having your heartbroken and then repaired.

I wanted a fictional story—only in real life—with a strong hero who would swoop in and fill my heart with joy. I sighed and looked around for Charlie. She was on the other side of the shop, leaning against the checkout with one hip and flirting with one of the employees.

Why couldn't I be more like her? I wanted to be outgoing, to be able to let go of my fear and forge on. Charlie touched the man's arm as she laughed, and I stood mesmerized as his smile widened, and he shifted slightly toward her. There was instant chemistry between those two, and I was in awe. I stood there for a full minute, watching them flirt with one another, and then finally, Charlie removed a card from her purse, took his hand, and placed the card into his palm.

They stared at one another, and then she tipped her dark head to the side, winked, and said she hoped to hear from him soon. She was grinning at me as she passed and glanced back over her shoulder once. I turned to the man, his gaze glued to her retreating back and a smile of amazement on his handsome face.

I wanted to stomp my foot, throw my hands in the air, and scream. She made it look so easy! How? How can she just walk up to a man and start talking, then give him her number? Seriously? I rushed after her and caught up to her on the sidewalk.

"How do you do that? You amaze me. If I could be a tenth as confident as you are, life would be so much easier."

"Ali, you don't give yourself enough credit. You are a confident person; you are an amazing person."

"Yeah, when I'm in the kitchen, but you can walk up to anyone, anywhere, and say anything. What were you two talking about anyway? He was a handsome man."

"Yes, he was. I told him I wanted him to model for me."

I snickered. "Did you tell him he was going to be nude when you did?"

She bumped her shoulder into mine as she laughed. "No, I didn't, and I wasn't even thinking that. I love his facial bone structure. I'd love to photograph him on the stairs of the museum."

Another thing I was in awe about with Charlie. She could see a person and immediately come up with the perfect backdrop for them. "You simply amaze me," I said with a sigh.

"Oh, Ali, you amaze me just as much. Especially when you cook one of your incredible desserts; that chocolate mousse thing that you made the other night—oh, my god, it was unbelievable."

"Ah, yes, Decadent Midnight, that's what I'm calling it. We are going to add it to the menu next month when we revamp it."

"It is going to be a bestseller."

"I hope so."

We finished our shopping and then stopped at a local pub for a drink and meal before we split ways. While we enjoyed a light dinner and drinks, we joked about our jobs, love, the past, and the future.

"I sure hope that it goes well for you this week. Will I be able to watch?"

"The dance sessions are closed, but they do have a viewing area for the recording of the dances on Friday for VIPs."

"Make sure my name is on that VIP list. I don't want to miss this!"

"Oh, I already have it there. I'm not sure I can do this without you being present."

Charlie hugged me tightly. "I know you don't have confidence in yourself, but I do for you. You can do this, Ali, I know you can."

"Thanks!" We said our goodbyes and parted ways on the street.

I stood under the overhang as she dashed down the street to the parking garage. I shifted my gaze up to the sky as the rain began to come down in torrents. Damn, I wish I had brought an umbrella. I considered hailing a cab, but it was only three blocks to my condo.

Crap, I sighed as I hunched forward and rushed out into the

rain. As I tried to avoid puddles on the sidewalk, I dwelled over the scene in the shop earlier. Would I ever find that instant kind of chemistry with someone? Would I be able to step up to a man and start a conversation that didn't revolve around sauces or blending or fresh produce?

I pursed my lips because I knew the answer—no.

I ducked around the corner and slammed right into someone, bouncing back and starting to lose my footing. A hand shot out, and the shopping bags dropped from my fingers as I clung to whatever I could.

I was jerked upright and stared into the tense features of the man who held me. His green eyes were drilling into me with an almost angry look—or was stressed. With a blink of the eyes, his features softened as his deep voice slithered down my spine. "Sorry, I wasn't looking where I was going."

I was practically struck mute—like I always was when an attractive man spoke to me—but I managed to nod and mutter, "Unexpected storm," as I memorized the shade of green in his eyes.

"Yeah, unexpected." He let go of me hastily and stepped around me to retrieve my bags as I stood there gawking. His hair was dark, and rivulets of water ran down his face—probably exactly how it was on mine. Oh man, I probably looked like a drowned rat!

Was it the rain or was his hair the same color as mine? It was cut short and showed off the cutest ears—and oh, how I wanted to touch them. His shoulders were broad, and as he turned back to me, I realized he was the perfect height. I loved men who were only a few inches taller than me. We could easily look into each others eyes, and there were never any awkward neck positions for either of us.

"Sorry," he said with a wince as he held the bags out to me, and I slowly took them, unable to tear my gaze from his. "You alright?" he asked abruptly.

I managed to nod, and then for two seconds, we stared at each other. I forgot about the rain, forgot about being soaked, or that my packages were probably ruined. In those brief moments, I saw things that I would never have expected to have seen. There was confusion, pain, and maybe even a little sorrow there, and it was like someone had just reached right into my chest and squeezed my heart.

A sharp ringing sound had me startling, and we broke eye contact as he reached into his pocket and pulled out a cellphone. He nodded at me and spun on his heel, taking long strides down the sidewalk and out of my life. Any chance of ever knowing more about him was gone, and I slowly turned and headed through the torrents of rain just as thunder vibrated overhead.

It was the story of my life.

CHAPTER THREE

HARVEY

I glanced back over my shoulder; the woman I'd practically trampled was turning the corner and now out of sight. I'd been lost in thought, shielding myself from the rain that came out of nowhere. With my head down, I hadn't been paying attention until I slammed into her. She'd had a silent beauty about her. One that radiated from deep within, but I didn't have time for that. A brother needed my help, and you never left a brother when they were in need. As I turned back around, I chalked it up to a missed opportunity and headed to the buddy's apartment.

* * *

MONDAY MORNING, I approached the building, glancing up at the sign above my head that read, Barbara Armand Dance Academy. What the hell was I doing here? Holly was lucky that I was here at all. Last night had been a nightmare. Todd, a close buddy of mine from the Marines, had one of his episodes, and several of us were there to talk him down and get him to take his meds.

I hadn't gotten home until almost four. Now at eight, as I pulled open the glass door and removed my shades, I had a feeling I wasn't going to like my reason for being here.

I took the stairs to the second floor as instructed and glanced around at the madhouse. People were milling about, with a ton of large plastic pelican cases and other hard equipment storage containers lining the hallway. What the hell was my sister filming, and why did she want me here?

It wasn't the first time that I had visited one of my sister's production sites, so it wasn't new to me, but I was still trying to figure out what was going on. What did my sister possibly need me here for? I knew nothing about dance or production. Maybe she had a star here and wanted some security. I glanced around the main room and down both hallways to locate my sister.

"Can you tell me where Holly Melton is?" I asked a woman as she began to pass me.

She pointed to the hallway on the right. "Second door on the right."

"Thanks," I told her as she hurried away.

As I stopped at the door, I heard my sister say, "I know he'll do it. He's my brother. He will do anything for me."

I rapped a knuckle on the door and stepped in. "Um, that might change depending on what you want me to do."

Holly turned bright eyes toward me. "Harv!" She threw her arms around my neck. "Thank you so much for coming."

"Yeah, well, I'm here. Now tell me why."

She winced slightly and glanced at the other man who had a wild beard and a baseball hat on backward, his arms covered in colorful ink.

"I'm filming this fun new show. It's a reality show." She paused and then spoke the next sentence in a rush. "The guy who was supposed to be in this episode was injured, and I needed a stand-in for him."

I laughed, never imagining myself on television. "You want me to be in one of your shows? Doing what? Am I just standing around, or do I have lines?"

The man beside her chuckled, and Holly slapped him in the chest with the back of her hand. "No speaking, well, there is some speaking, but what I really need you to do is dance."

I stared at her, then at the guy, and then turned my focus back to my sister as I cocked my head slightly. "Excuse me? What did you just say?"

She shook her dark hair back and lifted her chin. A clear sign that she was attempting to overcome her nerves. "I said I need you to dance."

I started laughing and glanced around a bit uncomfortably, wondering if my sister was trying to punk me. Were the cameras on already? "I swear you just said that you need me to dance."

"Yes, I did."

My jaw dropped as I stared at her in disbelief. "Are you crazy, Holly? I don't dance!"

She grabbed my arm as if she knew that the sudden urge to flee from the building was rushing through me. "Wait, Harvey, listen to what I have to say. Please! I really, really need your help. Please!" she begged, her voice getting all soft and sad, and it pissed me off because she knew what that did to me.

"I'm going to give you guys a few minutes," the other man said and then left, closing the door behind him.

"Why would you for one second think that this would be alright?"

"Oh, come on! It's not a big deal, Harv. They teach you a dance, and then you dance. You have fun, and then you go on with your life."

"Why are you asking me to do this? What the hell is this?"

She sighed wearily and took a seat. "It's called *May I Have*

This Dance. We take one person looking for love and match them with three compatible people. All of them learn the same dance, and then the one person, the female, in this case, dances with all three men—one of which will be you. You don't see each other until the music starts, and you don't even talk to one another. You just dance the routine, and when the music ends, you both walk away without a word."

I laughed. "And what the hell is the purpose of that?"

"Well, these people are looking for love, for a connection with the other person; they are searching for chemistry."

I laughed harder and crossed my arms over my chest. "You think that people can find love dancing with strangers and never saying a word? I know you are flighty and romantic, Holly, but this is stupid even for you."

She lurched forward into my face. "This is not stupid, Harvey! This is a chance for someone to find love. It means something to someone—to me—to them. I don't expect her to choose you—you are far from her type—but I needed someone safe to fill the spot. The guy who was supposed to be here broke his damn leg, and our process to get on this show is intense and has a lot of background checks. I know you're good and that you aren't some crazy lunatic, so that's why I asked you."

I grunted.

She took me by the shoulders and gave me her damn puppy dog eyes. "Please, Harvey. I needed someone quick, and you are the only person I can count on."

"Do I really have to dance?"

"Yes, but I have a great choreographer that is going to help, and two professional dancers that are going to assist you in learning the routine."

"Why can't one of them do it?"

"Because I need someone real, who doesn't have professional experience, and who is handsome and *could* be her type."

"What is her name?"

"I can't tell you that."

"What?"

"I can't tell you her name, and she won't know yours or the other two men either. You won't even talk to her; you'll just dance and then walk away."

"How long does this take, Holly? I only have the week off from work."

"It's just a week. You'll work on the dance for four days, and on Friday, you'll have your date with her."

"Date?"

"Dance date."

"And that's it?"

"Yes, that's it." She nodded quickly. "The other two men are totally her type, so I doubt she'll pick you."

I stared down at my sister, taking in the same green eyes that I had. "What if by some odd chance she does pick me; what happens then?"

My sister chuckled. "Oh, don't worry, she won't, but if for some weird reason she did, then you'd have to learn another dance, and do it one more time."

I glanced around the room, inhaling deeply with my hands on my hips. "Man, are you going to owe me for doing this. Do you have any idea how much the guys are going to get on my case for this?"

"You don't have to tell them." She winced. "Well, they might hear about it once it goes on television."

I groaned and stared at the ceiling. "Fine, fine. I'll do this, but damn it, Holly, you are going to owe me something fierce."

She squealed and threw herself into my arms. "Thank you so much, Harvey. I knew I could count on you!" She pulled back, grabbing my arm. "Okay, let's get you to makeup."

"Makeup?"

"Yeah." She glanced at me, her eyes drifting over my face.

"Yeah, you don't need much, just a bit to even out your tone and highlight your eyes."

"Holly, if you tell any of the guys that I work with that you put makeup on me, I'm going to kill you."

"Don't worry, no one will know."

"Famous last words," I muttered to myself as I followed her into the next room.

As I sat in the chair, a woman with wild red hair turned my face left and then right, and another woman fiddled with my hair, while my sister and a third woman went through the paperwork with me. There was one disclaimer after another, and I signed my name a dozen times that I wouldn't sue the production company, the dance company, any of the film crew, the city, or the female co-star for any reason.

It all seemed ridiculous to me, but I went through the motions for my sister. When we finished, and they said I was ready, I looked in the mirror and wanted to laugh. My face had never looked so even and smooth, and the eye makeup that they put on me did make the green stand out a little more.

I can't believe I'm wearing freaking makeup. Holy shit! The only makeup I'd ever worn in my life was camouflage for operations.

Holly introduced me to a few more people, including the host, and then they explained what I would be doing. The host knew that I was standing in but told me to come up with a story on why I would want to do this. It was something that they asked every contestant, and I was at a loss. I guess I'd say the first thing that came to mind.

The filming began with me coming into the dance studio and meeting the choreographer and dancers. When Tarin, the host, asked me why I wanted to find love, I answered immediately.

"At my age, it's hard to find someone who wants the same things that I do. I'm hoping that this might be my chance."

Tarin seemed thrilled with my answer, and the ball kept rolling. We'd stop and start things over and over again during questions and explanations, but then we came to the point that it was time for me to start learning the dance.

"This is the song that you are going to dance to." She pushed a button, and the song began to play.

I stared to laugh. "Yeah, I know this one. It was popular when it came out."

"Yes! *Shut Up and Dance* by Walk the Moon is perfect! So full of energy, and it will totally be able to bring you two close and see if the energy is there between you without being too intimate."

"Alright, let's do this," I said, sounding way more excited than I felt. What was I doing here? This was the craziest thing I had ever done, and I was already trying to figure out what I could ask Holly to do in return—equally crazy.

They showed me the dance routine, and the temptation to turn and walk—no run—out of the room was filling me rapidly. When I glanced at Holly, she looked tense, as if she expected me to do just that.

Man, I did not want to do this, but I would—for her. I really would do anything for her; I was putty in her hands.

"Well, what do you think?" Tarin asked me with barely concealed excitement in her light-brown eyes as the dancers finished. I glanced around the room and tried not to let my panic show through.

"I think that we have a lot of work to do." I swear I heard Holly release the air from her lungs. Yeah, I didn't want to do this, but I gave her my word. Now I needed to bite the bullet and make it through the landmine with my masculinity in check.

Cal, the choreographer, stated with jubilance, "Let's get started! Before the music begins, you're going to walk up to the corner of the building, and this prop wall right here represents that. You're going to lean back against it casually as if you don't have a care in the world. Like you are just waiting for someone to come along and she will be on the other side. Then the music starts."

He put me in position and had Clara, my female dancer, stand around the corner from me. "Put your foot up behind you, lean back, look relaxed. You'll be wearing jeans in this, so maybe tuck your thumbs into your pockets."

I chuckled to myself as I tried to do as they asked.

"Okay, so the music starts, and you're going to count, one, two, three, and then you are going to peek around the corner slightly. You'll see her, but she's looking away from you, and then you slip back on seven, eight. That's when she will turn her face toward the corner. Another one, two, and you're going to put your hand out like this." Cal held his hand up as if I would have a tray on it, only more relaxed. "That's three and four. On five and six, she will put her hand into yours, and on seven, eight, you will push off the wall, step out, and pull her into you. She's going to spin toward you and end with her back to your chest. Let's try that so far."

We went slowly through the motions twice, counting aloud, and then we did it a second time, and I counted the beats to myself.

"Okay, in this next part, you're going to run your hand down her side, take her other hand, and then spin her out."

I laughed, spiking a brow. "You want me to run my hand down the side of a woman I've never even met, along her rib cage?"

"Yep, this is a moment when she has to trust you; she wants to feel wanted and attractive, and then you spin her out, and she comes back to you. Now she's facing you, and this is where you two get your first eye contact. When you gaze down at her, you want her to see you, see right into your soul. You want her to fall a little in love with you in that very second."

The last thing I wanted was any woman looking right into my dark soul. Oh, hell, no! The second to last thing that I wanted was any woman to fall in love with me. I peered sideways at my sister wishing that I could walk the hell out of here, but instead, we took it from the top.

CHAPTER FOUR

ALI

$\mathcal{M}$onday afternoon, I arrived at the dance academy and bounced up the steps. I bubbled with an energy that I hadn't felt in a long time, and although I was scared to death of what I was going to do, I was excited too.

I located Holly quickly as I reached the second-floor lobby area, and she rushed to my side and hugged me tightly. "I am so glad that I got you on the show, Ali. You are going to have so much fun, and I know you are going to find someone to love during this—I just know it!"

"Honestly, I can't believe I let you talk me into applying for it, but now that I'm doing it, I'm excited. Nervous as a cat in a room full of rocking chairs, but still excited."

Holly laughed. We had met a year ago when her production crew had come into the restaurant where I was working for an end of the season party. She had asked to speak to the chef, and I'd come out to the private room where she and forty other people raved over the meal. Holly and I had clicked immediately when she asked if it was cardamom that she tasted in the rice.

A few days later, Holly was back at the restaurant early, and I took a break, sharing a new dish with her. She soon became my favorite taste tester and friend. We didn't hang out often, but she was always bringing her friends into the restaurant. Being a chef, I worked long hours from mid-afternoon until almost midnight, so I missed the regular hanging out times.

I didn't mind, I love my job, and I enjoyed the fact that Holly came by the restaurant and was willing to try out new concoctions. I valued and trusted her opinion.

"If you are nervous now, just wait until Friday when you get ready for your dance dates."

"Oh, my god! Don't remind me, Holly. It's too early in the week to pass out!"

She grinned as she spoke and hooked her arm with mine. "Come on, let's get you to makeup. No passing out; you'll be fine."

After a whirlwind of makeup and hair, I returned to the studio, and we started taping. For the first few minutes, I was extremely uncomfortable knowing the camera was on me but was able to put it out of my mind pretty quickly. The only time that I was reminded they were there was when they wanted us to redo something from a different angle.

When Tarin turned on the music, I laughed, and Cal stood in front of me. "This is a bold song, full of energy. You're telling these men to prove themselves without words. To show you that you can trust them and that they can be there for you and that you can both have fun."

"I can't believe I'm doing this!"

"Do you want to see the routine?"

"Yes, show me what kind of trouble I'm getting myself into."

I watched the dance with ever-widening eyes. I was out of breath by the time the dance routine finished, and I wasn't doing anything but watching. How the heck was I going to be able to do that, not once, but three times with three different men?

"What do you think?"

"Holy—cow! It's fun and sexy and full of energy, and then there are moments when it can be so much more."

Cal clapped. "Yes! That is exactly what we are looking for. Are you ready to get started, Ali?"

"My knees are shaking, but yes, I'm ready to get started."

As Cal, and Victor, my dance partner for training, showed me the first few steps, I thought briefly of the man I'd run into coming around the corner the other night in the storm. Is that what this was going to feel like? Would the electrifying moment when we look into each other's eyes be as intense as that moment had been?

A second later, that thought was gone, and I was waist-deep in counting beats, kicks, turns, hips swivels, and body waves.

"Ali, when you look at him here, you want to take a moment to let him in. You're not just trying to find out more about him, but you are allowing him into your soul. You want him to see that you are this incredibly loving and sincere person. Since it's so hard for you to talk to strangers, you have to let your body do it for you."

I couldn't imagine my body telling anyone anything, but I wanted it to. I genuinely hoped that this whole experiment worked. For it to do that, I had to give it my all. "Okay, if you say so."

"Let's try it again."

It ended up taking another four times before Cal and Tarin clapped their hands excitedly. "Yes! That right there showed your vulnerability; it was perfect!"

"That is crazy scary," I told them.

"Oh, there is no doubt that it is," Tarin said. "It is frightening to open yourself up to strangers and let them see the real you, but it's going to pay off."

"I hope so."

Tarin took my hands. "I know so!"

"And cut!" someone called from off to the side.

"That's a wrap for today," Holly said and approached us. "How are you feeling, Ali?"

"Good! I'm excited, and I do love this dance, but I'm exhausted too."

She chuckled as I glanced at the clock on the far wall. "Oh, no! I need to get going. I'm already late to work. I told them I'd be a couple of hours late, but eek, I'm later than I thought I would be!"

"Go, we will see you tomorrow, and you did fantastic!"

I gave Holly a quick hug. "Thank you, Holly."

I rushed out of the studio, grabbed my things, and was out on the street in a moment. I could walk, but it would take a while and only make me later. Instead, I hailed a cab, and even though I wasn't a fan of using them, I didn't feel so uncomfortable today as I slipped into the back seat and gave the driver the address to Randolph's, the restaurant where I worked as the head chef.

While I was later than expected, but only by thirty minutes, and I knew my kitchen staff would have everything under control. I'd told them that I might be a little late today, and they all knew what I was doing. When I had explained it, I had gotten some good-natured ribbing, but I didn't mind. The other employees in the kitchen were my friends and family. If you couldn't joke around with them, who could you joke with? When I arrived, I rushed down the alley beside the restaurant and came in from the back.

It was only three-thirty in the afternoon, and the restaurant didn't open on Monday's until five, but the cooking was fully underway. Desserts were being prepared, bases and stocks were on the stove for the main dishes. The vegetables were being washed and cut.

I slipped into our small employee lounge and changed out of my leggings and t-shirt to my chef's pants and coat. I wasn't too worried about the fact that I was sweaty from dancing. Five minutes near the stove during rush hour dinner, and I'd be ten times worse.

"Hey, hey!" Ricardo, my sous chef, called as I stepped into the kitchen. "The star is here. How did your dance lesson go today?"

I laughed. "I'm hardly a star, Ricardo."

"Ah, but you are. You, my Chef de Cuisine, are a bright and shining star. If I were not the man I am, I would be interested in a woman as beautiful as you."

I stared at Ricardo. "I'm going to take that as a compliment, and try not to ask you why you are buttering me up."

He laughed. "You picked up on that, didn't you?"

"Yes, so what's wrong?"

"The cod that you wanted for tomorrow night's special will not be available. They called today and said there was a problem with their main fishing boat, and they couldn't meet the demand this week."

"That's the second time that they have done that." I tied my apron around my waist. "Fine, I think we might need to source out a new vendor for some of our fish."

"Might not be a bad idea," Ricardo said. "In the meantime, we can get tilapia; I already checked with that supplier to see if they can get it in. They said it wasn't a problem if we told them by five tonight."

I winced and glanced at the clock. "Better get on it, then."

"Yes, Chef." Ricardo hustled away to make the call, and I scanned the kitchen.

I had started here as a Sauté Chef seven years ago. Three years after I started, I moved up to the Sous Chef position, and last year, I took over the Head Chef position, when Monty decided to retire. Despite the title, the Head Chef didn't usually do as much cooking as many of the other chefs, but I preferred to have my hands in it all. Maybe that was a bit controlling, but I didn't think the others in the kitchen minded. I knew Ricardo didn't, and since he was my right-hand man, I appreciated that.

There were thirteen of us that worked in the kitchen. I was the top of the food chain, Ricardo, right beneath me. Behind him was Paul, my Sauté chef, who was responsible for sautéing foods and creating the sauces and gravies that went with other dishes.

Then came Maryanne, who was our Boucher, our meat chef, and she was in charge of all meats, including fish, although she didn't deal with roasting, frying, or grilling. Maryanne made sure the meats were cleaned, prepared, marinated, and ready to be cooked by the other chefs.

Malick was our Rotisseur or our Roast Chef, and he was responsible for all the roasted meats and sauces while Ben was our Friturier or our Fry Chef. Anything fried was his to oversee.

We also had a Grillardin, a Grill Chef, and Nate worked that position, always trying new rubs and spices on the grilled meats and vegetables.

Josiah was our Garde Manager, more often known as the Pantry Chef who prepared the cold dishes and salads, and we had Tobias, the jack of all trades as the Chef de Tounant. He moved around the kitchen as needed and knew enough about every position to get by without being dangerous.

We had an Entremetier, who was responsible for all the vegetables, and Melinda worked that station. Her boyfriend, Wallace, was our Junior Chef. He was still in culinary school, and he was lucky to land this position to keep up his training.

The last two people in our hectic kitchen were Sadie and David. Sadie was our Kitchen Porter, responsible for prep work, and usually one of the first to arrive each day, while David was our Exuelerie. A fancy term for dishwasher, but not just a dishwasher. He was responsible for making sure our kitchen tools were well maintained, cleaned, and ready for use. He also let us know when something was amiss with a tool and needed to be replaced.

Josiah and Tobias were our two newest members, having

recently replaced a couple of guys who were caught stealing from the kitchen. So far, they were working out, and the kitchen was running like clockwork.

This place was my sanctuary, my haven. Here, I was intense but also vibrant and confident. If only I could meet someone here that I could fall in love with—someone who understood what long hours meant, what sacrifice meant to do something that you loved.

My last relationship had ended because of my job. Thomas had said that I always put my career first, that I'd rather be in my kitchen than making love to him. I can't say that he was wrong. I mean, I did care about him, and I did enjoy our time together, but when I was in the kitchen, I forgot about everything else. Nothing else mattered, and I did become neglectful of him and our relationship. Was that because of my job or because he wasn't the right man for me?

Maybe if I found the man that I was supposed to be with, then perhaps I wouldn't lose myself in cooking, or menus, or searching for the right supplier. Maybe, I'd be more interested in lying in bed, making love for hours, or having him cook me a meal. Something I'd never let Thomas do—well, not after the first time. Thomas prepared a meal for me once, but when I saw that he was using a jar sauce for the pasta, I almost kicked him out of his own kitchen. After that, I'd let him assist, but even that was difficult, because I had my way of doing things, and I expected him to do them that way.

I glanced at Paul, who was at the stove, preparing a large stock base for tonight. Oddly enough, I didn't critique the people in this kitchen the way I did in my personal kitchen. Here, everyone had a style, a form of doing things, and I accepted that—appreciated it really. It was only in my own home that I tended to be overbearing and controlling when it came to how things should be done. Don't get me wrong; I wasn't shy to let one of my chefs know if something wasn't up to par.

Would I ever find a man who didn't think they were competing with my job? Or who could stand being in the kitchen with me while I cooked? I wasn't sure, but I did hope so. Maybe this week, I'd find that man, a man who was independent, confident, kind, and didn't need me to make him feel more like a man just by being at his side.

I might like to cook, but the last thing I wanted was an overbearing man who expected me barefoot and pregnant in the kitchen. Okay, well, maybe barefoot and pregnant would be okay as long as he knew I was coming back to work.

CHAPTER FIVE

HARVEY

I was running late, and I hated being late. Not that I had to be there for this lunch or meeting, but because I wanted to. I was looking forward to seeing what Maggie was going to do for our company, and quite honestly, I had nothing else to do with my afternoon.

I had been working for Jake for just over a year, and I had two weeks of vacation to burn. The next few months were filled with training and trips, so I decided to use my time while I could. I thought about borrowing Mike's cabin on the lake, but since Maggie and Greg had been using that place for the last five weeks, I figured that Mike probably wanted the cabin to himself for a little while.

Although Mike was working all week, so maybe I could have gone up for a few days. That could have been nice, except I didn't have anyone to go with me.

The last woman I dated, Sherry, broke it off about seven months ago. I thought things were going well, but I guess she didn't like me traveling all over the world and only being home half the month—or less.

I had been married twice. My first wife and I married when we were only twenty, and she ended up hating the military lifestyle and left me to return home while I was on deployment three years into our marriage. I'd received one of those famous Dear John letters while I was in Iraq, and it had almost broken my heart—almost.

My next wife was four years later and lasted for five years. I thought we had a great thing going, but when I came home on leave and surprised her, the shock was on me, as I found her in our bed with her boss.

Since my second marriage ended, I'd dated a handful of women, but I couldn't say that I'd been all in with any of them. I figured that after two failed attempts, the chances of finding anyone now were slim. Most women either had their families or had their careers.

Although I wanted a wife to come home to and had always hoped for a couple of children, I didn't expect that now, and I was upfront with every woman that I met. I'd love to have a great time, but I wasn't sure that I was looking for anything long term. I even explained to them that my job came first, and I traveled a lot. I never asked them to wait for me, never asked them to be monogamous, and so far, it was good. A bit lonely at times, and Holly got on my case often, but I was okay with that.

Maybe that was contradictory, wanting a family, and telling women that I wasn't in it for the long haul. I guess if I ever found the right woman, I would change the way I thought, but I wasn't holding out for that.

I pulled into our training facility and saw Joe and Wyatt off to the side of the lot smoking. "You know those things will kill you," I said to them as I passed by.

"So will a gun, but you still shoot them," Wyatt replied with a laugh.

That was kind of the mentality with all of us. Something was going to kill us, might as well enjoy the ride while you can. Although I tended to be the extreme one in the group, and by extreme, I didn't mean the one that did all the unhealthy things. No, I was the opposite.

My body was my temple, and I only put the best into it—except beer. Beer was always allowed to enter the temple. I worked out, ate right, scheduled physicals, took vitamins, got my teeth cleaned twice a year. I made sure to get enough sleep—most of the time—and felt like I was twenty-five and not turning forty.

Most of the people were still sitting around the table in the classroom area, but Trevor was piling food on his plate. "Hey, man, you just get here?" I asked as I collected a plate and glanced over the spread.

"Yeah, Devon had a checkup this morning, ran a little late," he said as Alice reached past me and grabbed a pickle spear off the plate. She glanced at me and then did a double take.

I hiked a brow at her as she leaned toward me. "Are you wearing makeup?"

Ah, shit! I had forgotten to get that cleaned off when we finished. Holy crap!

"Makeup?" Trevor jumped in with a laugh. "Are you?"

"No, I am not."

Alice got closer to me. "Oh, you most certainly are! Why are you wearing makeup?"

"It's no big deal, Alice. I forgot to wipe it off."

"Why are you wearing it in the first place?" Trev asked before he turned to the group behind him. "Hey, our man is wearing makeup over here."

I wanted to turn and bang my head against the wall as people started laughing and throwing out comments. Joe and Wyatt took that moment to return and asked what was going on.

"Explain, Melton!" Alex said with a laugh. "If you don't explain the reasonable explanation that you are totally trying to come up with at this very moment, you are going to be ruined for life."

This was the last thing that I wanted. Wait till I got my hands on my sister—gah! "There is a very reasonable explanation for it."

"You have a new gig as a cross-dresser?" Jake asked with a smirk.

"Funny, no, that's Joe's other job."

"Hey, I only did that twice. It was fun, and man, the tips were damn good."

"So, what's with the makeup?" Jake approached me and ran his gaze over my face after he grabbed hold of my chin. "Your eyes are so pretty."

I slapped his hand away and growled, "Get your hands off me, you ass."

"You know, I might be new to this group, but I don't think you're going to live this down until you explain," Maggie said softly beside me and handed me a hoagie.

"What's this?"

"Had it made especially for you. Whole wheat with turkey and loaded with veggies, dry."

I leaned forward and kissed her cheek. "You are the best. When you get tired of Blaire, you let me know."

She laughed as Greg yelled from the table that he heard that. I added a little fruit salad to my plate and a couple of pretzels, grabbed a bottle of green tea, and went to take a seat.

"Nope, you can't sit here until you explain about the make-up," Drake said and then studied me carefully. "Your eyes really do stand out more now, though."

"Jesus, guys, I'm on a television show, alright? It's no big deal; I'm just helping my sister out last minute, and they wanted my skin even and to make my eyes pop. We were running late, and I forgot to remove it. Okay? Everyone understands now, right?"

People were looking at one another, and then Greg leaned

back in his seat, crossing his arms as he smirked. "Depends on what show it is that you are on."

Ah, shit! I wanted to hang my head, but I didn't.

Greg continued. "See, because I know for a fact that your sister is working on a new television show about finding love while dancing."

"Wait! Who is your sister?" Maggie asked quickly, her eyes wide and excited.

There was no out here—none, zip, zilch, zero. "Holly Melton, the producer."

Maggie giggled. "Oh, I love Holly! I interviewed her for my romance column. I thought the idea of that show was fantastic! That's so funny; I was just talking to Greg about it the other day." She turned to Greg. "Why didn't you tell me that he was her brother?"

Greg began to laugh, and then he was laughing so hard he was crying. His actions started everyone else laughing just because Greg was making such an ass of himself. I sat down and proceeded to eat, pretending like nothing was wrong.

"Your—" He kept on cackling. "Dancing!" He swiped at his eye, his hand on his stomach like it was trying to keep it from bursting. "Oh, my god! You're dancing for love!" He howled, and that just got everyone else going harder. Before I knew it, I was chuckling, and then as the jokes began to explode around the room, I sat there and laughed till I cried. Maggie handed me a napkin to wipe the makeup off my cheeks, and that just got everyone laughing more.

By the time we got settled down, my stomach was cramping from laughter, and my cheeks ached from smiling. I hadn't laughed this damn hard in so long, and god, after last night, I needed it, too.

Maggie sat down next to me. "So, you're a contestant?"

"I'm a stand-in."

She frowned. "So you aren't competing for a second date?"

I shook my head. "No, Holly said I wasn't this girl's type. I only did it to help my sister. She was in a bind because one of the guys broke his leg water-skiing."

"But what if you do it and find out that you like the girl? Are you going to do a second dance?"

I shrugged. "I have no clue. Until eight this morning, I didn't know I was doing this one."

Most everyone started asking questions about it, and after the first few, Maggie began answering them. I did not miss the fact that this woman knew a hell of a lot more about what I was getting myself into, and I listened intently.

"What's the dance look like?" Joe asked.

"Why? You want to be my partner?"

"Well, you do look awful sexy with that smeared makeup on. Let me take your picture."

"Don't you dare." I reached for his phone, and he jumped back.

"Alright, guys!" Jake stood up to get everyone's attention. "Let's clean up a bit and get moving. We will all be sure to watch Harv make a fool out of himself later."

I was still eating, but others cleaned up and then got seated while Mike set things up on the big screen and logged into our new website that was going live soon. It looked clean and welcoming, but also business-like and patriotic, too. Maggie, Jake, and Mike took turns talking about different aspects of the website and what they hope to add soon, including more training, photographs, and bios about all the instructors. Although for safety reasons, they wouldn't be too extensive. That information could be shared during classes and meetings like we usually did now.

Then they started showing off the videos that Maggie had been creating. They were fantastic. Not only did Maggie work up a great video about the delivery of the medical supplies that we had done a few weeks ago, but she had also done a few others.

Jake had collected a bunch of random videos that we'd shared with him, and she had compiled a fantastic five-minute video of us doing different things. From training to travel, and even some of our more stressful moments when we were under fire, and civilians were put to work to show what they learned.

A couple of the guys whistled when it was over, and Alex spoke up. "I just want to make it known that while I absolutely love what Maggie has done, and I honestly do. I have been trying to get Jake to do these things for months!"

A bunch of us laughed as Jake replied, "Yeah, well, who wants to listen to you jack-jawing. Maggie is much easier to listen to."

Greg snorted. "That's not what you said to me the other night."

"Wait! What?" Maggie spun on Jake. "You said I wasn't nice to listen to?"

Jake's features went dead serious as he put his hand to his chest. "Never."

"Bullshit!" Greg crowed. "You said that if you had to listen to one more thing that Maggie wanted to change, you were going to go nuts!"

Maggie's jaw dropped. "I thought you liked my ideas."

Jake came to stand in front of her. "I do! I do, Maggie. I love your ideas; we just don't need to do all of them in the first month you are working here."

For a second, I thought she would cry, and Jake looked like he was going to freak, but at the last second, she giggled. "Okay, fine, I'll slow down my ideas. It's just nice to be taken seriously."

"You got it." Jake looked so relieved, and then serious as he glanced my way. "Although we are going to need to update Harvey's profile to read professional dancer."

"I'm never going to hear the end of this."

Alice stepped around me, patting my back, and stopped next to Maggie. "See what I have to deal with all the time?"

Maggie put her hand on Alice's shoulder. "I feel for you, I honestly do. At least you aren't the only woman in the office anymore."

"That is an excellent thing. I was about to lose my mind with all these men."

"I got your back, Alice."

"It's I got your six," I said to Maggie.

She smiled at me. "Yes, that is what you military people say, but us pure-blooded civilians say, I got your back."

"Yeah, okay," I replied with a snicker.

Alice took a seat next to me. "So what was it like?"

"What?"

She rolled her eyes. "The dance show, you idiot."

I shrugged as Maggie took a seat beside me to listen. "I guess it was alright. I mean, I was only there for a few hours, and we started taping immediately and learning the dance."

"Yeah, you think you'll be any good?" Maggie asked.

"No." I smirked her way. "I suck at dancing. I've never been into it."

"Ah, my daddy used to say that if you want to win a woman's heart, learn how to take her around the dance floor," Alice said almost dreamily.

"Seriously?" I asked her. "Do women seriously like men who dance?"

"Yes!" Maggie and Alice replied in unison.

Maggie grinned at Alice. "Jinx. There is something so damn sexy about a man who can dance. They don't even have to dance well, as long as they can make a woman feel special."

I rested my elbows on the table, oddly interested in what she was saying. "How do you make a woman feel special when you dance?"

"Look her in the eye, hold her tight. If your hand is on her lower back, rub her spine with your thumb."

Alice continued. "Lead her, don't let her lead you. Make sure to take charge, stand up straight, and don't be soft—but don't be a Neanderthal either. Women like strong men who are in control on the dance floor."

"Do they?" I said with mock-seriousness, and Drake, who had taken a seat next to Alice, grinned.

"Don't get all smart-assed with me, buddy. You asked. We are just trying to help you find love on the dance floor," Alice said.

"I told you that I'm only doing this for my sister. I have no intention of finding love or even lust."

Alice turned to Drake. "Famous last words, huh, Drake?"

Drake nodded. "Yep. He's toast."

"Whatever. If you all don't mind, I'm going to get out of here and go enjoy my week off."

"Alright, twinkle toes," Trevor said as he slapped me on the back. "You have fun. You might want to ask Maggie or Alice what they use to take their makeup off at night. Don't want it to clog your pores."

I shoved Trevor away. "Get out of my face, moron."

CHAPTER SIX

ALI

*I*t was Wednesday, and I was exhausted and sore—like everywhere. After spending two days working muscles and contorting my body in ways that it hadn't moved in years for several hours, and then rushing to work and spending another ten hours on my feet, I was whipped. My lower back ached, my feet throbbed, and all I wanted to do was find a spa and get a full body massage and spa treatment.

Sadly, that wasn't in the cards as I worked on the dance routine once more. I pretty much had it down pat, and I was getting more excited—and a whole lot more nervous. As Cal talked to someone about a change, I wondered if any of the men I was about to dance date with liked to go to the spa?

Cal returned to Victor and me and said to take a break. I thought about how tomorrow's practice would be shorter as we went to the actual location of the dance, and then we'd run through it there to make sure that I had it down, and they could make any changes for the location and environment that might need to be made. I would only have time to run through it a couple of times before I'd be rushed from the location so that the men could practice.

I couldn't believe that it was almost time for my dancing dates. I was still a little in awe of the fact that I had even agreed to do this. I stood on the side of the studio, sipping from my water bottle, when Holly joined me. "Off-camera, how are you holding up?"

I chuckled. "I like how you said off-camera."

"Yeah, I know, on-camera, we want you to be all excited and positive, but this is your friend asking you how you are doing, not the producer."

"I'm nervous!" I blurted out. "Like crazy nervous, but excited too, and my entire body hurts." I held my pinkie up. "Except my pinkie, it doesn't hurt—yet!"

We laughed. "Yeah, my body would be too if I was doing the things that Cal has you doing. I have to tell you that I love the part where you get on the park wall, and you are all sassy and in their face. You do that so well, and it's like the real you is finally getting a chance to come out and play."

"It's funny that you say that. That is one of my favorite parts too. It just feels so fun and playful, but it's also where I suddenly get nervous again because I have to trust them to pick me up over their head and not drop me."

"Yes, that is very true, but you can trust these men. I promise they are just as worried about dropping you as you are concerned that they will."

"Do you honestly think that I'll make a connection, Holly? I mean, do you think it's possible?"

"Well, the last four contestants that we had all did."

"Did they? You're not just saying that? They sincerely found a connection?"

"I'm not just saying that." She made an *X* over her heart and then glanced at her watch. "You ready to get back to it? We are going to do a bit of question and answer before we run you through it one last time today."

"Let's get going." My cellphone began to ring and I glanced

at it to see Ricardo was calling me. He never called me unless it was imperative. "Wait, Holly, I need to take this, can you give me two minutes?"

"Sure." She stepped away to speak with Tarin and Cal.

"You caught me during a break, but I only have two minutes. What's up, Ricardo?"

"Someone got sick," he stated, and I frowned.

"Okay, so move Tobias into the position, that's why we have a swing chef, and Wallace can help him."

"No, Ali, a customer got sick."

"What?"

"The health department is here right now. They said that a customer got sick on our food."

"Are you serious?"

"Yes, they said they need to speak to you immediately. Ali, it's E. coli."

I glanced at the crew and then Tarin, Holly, Cal, and Victor, who stood waiting for me.

"Ali, did you hear me? The health department needs to speak to you immediately!"

"Yes! Yes, I heard you. Give me a couple of minutes, and I'll be on my way. How was it possibly E. coli? We clean above standards!"

"I don't know, just get here, Ali."

"I'm on my way," I said and then rushed to Holly. "I have to leave."

"What? You can't leave; we aren't finished taping for the day."

"Holly, the Department of Health is in my kitchen right now, and they are doing a surprise inspection because they received a report that someone got sick in our restaurant. I have to go. I have no choice! I can try to meet you all earlier tomorrow if that works."

I was already backing away as they stared after me, and then

Holly nodded. "Go! Yes, that's important. I'll reach out to you later."

"Thanks, Holly, and I'm so sorry!" I grabbed my stuff and was running down the stairs and out to the street. I didn't even hesitate to catch a cab, and the whole time, a million questions ran through my mind. What had he eaten? Who had prepared it? How had it gotten contaminated? In all my years of cooking, I had never had something like this happen to me. I'd seen it happen to other chefs and watched what they went through. Some had been fined, some fired, a few kitchens closed and businesses destroyed, all because of a single complaint.

I felt sick to my stomach as the taxi came to a stop, and I passed money over to the driver and fled the cab. I walked with my head up, my shoulders back, trying to appear confident and not scared to death. My entire career could be at stake with this one instance. My reputation for keeping a clean, efficient kitchen could be destroyed.

I paused at the back door, inhaled slowly, and released it before pulling open the door. Inside, a few of the kitchen staff milled around by the door. All of them turned to me with wide, worried eyes. They knew, like me, what could be lost with this. "Have they found anything?" I asked Paul in a whisper.

He shook his head. "They just started the main kitchen inspection. They finished the dishwashing area."

"Okay, why don't all of you head outside. Ask everyone else to hang out there until they are done."

"Will do, Chef."

"Melinda, can you take my bag and put it in the locker room, please?"

"Yes, Chef." I stopped at the sink right inside the kitchen and washed my hands. It was the first thing I did when I stepped into this room and something that I required all my staff to do also.

"Hello, I'm Ali Davidson, Head Chef. I understand that a customer filed a complaint of an E. coli infection."

"Hello, Ms. Davidson. Jim Rushmore, Department of Health Inspector, and yes, a customer filed a complaint after spending the morning in the emergency room. They confirmed the bacteria in his system was E. coli."

"Was it E. coli O157:H7?

"Yes."

"And when did he state he ate here?"

"Last night."

I frowned. "That's almost impossible for him to have symptoms that quickly. The incubation period is generally more than twenty-four hours, and sometimes doesn't manifest for a few days."

Mr. Rushmore pursed his lips at me. "You don't need to quote those facts to me, Ms. Davidson. I am well aware of the symptoms and period for the bacteria to take effect."

I cringed at his stern tone. "Can you tell me what he ate?"

"He consumed a garden salad, Steak Au Poivre, and crepes with fresh berries and cream for dessert."

Well, crap! There were a lot of places the E. coli could have been hiding in that menu. However, I was still bothered by the fact that he was struck so quickly with symptoms.

"What has been tested so far?"

"The dishwasher and sanitizing area is clean, and we are about halfway through this area. We'll need to test the foods next. I will need to know how many salads you served last night, how many of the steaks, and how many dessert dishes you brought out to patrons."

"Yes, of course." I turned to Ricardo. "Can you please get the numbers?"

"Yes, Chef." He disappeared toward the office. While our numbers for salads were sometimes off, we would have a general number on that. Some people who ordered didn't want their salad or switched it with another one of our salads instead of the standard garden. The number for the steaks would be exact though.

Ricardo returned a few minutes later as I stood off to the side and watched every move the two inspectors took. "Chef," Ricardo handed me a piece of paper that he printed out. Ricardo had not only given me last night's numbers but the night before too.

"Thank you, Ricardo. Is this since our last meat delivery?" He nodded, and I handed the document to Mr. Rushmore, and he looked it over.

"We'll notify the local hospitals to be on the lookout for more cases. If it was in the salad, you could have hundreds of cases."

"If it was in the salad, but I still don't think it was from us. Was this man healthy otherwise?"

"As far as I know."

"Was it possible he had a compromised immune system? That is the only way I can see him turning ill so quickly. It hasn't even been twenty-four hours. Do you know the odds of that?"

He rolled his eyes. "Yes, I know the odds, Ms. Davidson. I've been doing this for a very long time."

"Okay, and how often have you seen someone come down with E. coli poisoning in less than twenty-four hours?"

He pursed his lips and turned away from me, saying over his shoulder, "it can happen."

His response meant that it had never happened in his career, and now my kitchen reputation was at stake. The fact that they were here was already a taint to our shining rep. It would show up on their site by tonight that they were investigating us for E. coli. Plus, it would be put into the paper to announce, in case someone else got sick, but not bad enough to go to the hospital. They will want to track all the claims, and they will have to weed out the people who are trying to screw us by making a buck in a lawsuit—a lawsuit! Oh, my god!

I squeezed my eyes closed; I had to call Randolph and let him know what was going on before he heard about it through another chef. What time was it in France right now? I glanced at my watch; it was just after three here, and France was six hours ahead so it would only be nine there. He would be at his brother's restaurant, probably cooking, so I'd wait at least another hour, or two, and then call him.

It was just after four, and they had tested every surface in our kitchen. We were seriously behind in preparing, and the kitchen was a madhouse. Luckily, my staff was professional and calm, and the minute they said we could return to the kitchen, everything started moving in super—but safe—speeds.

I sat at the desk in the back office and stared at the international phone number for Randolph. My gaze shifted to the report in front of me, and I was glad that Mr. Rushmore hadn't found anything in his inspection. It made me even more confident that the person had gotten sick elsewhere.

I picked up the desk phone and started to dial the number. It took a few seconds to connect, and then it was ringing. A woman's voice answered and spoke too quickly for me to understand. While I did know some French, it was reserved for simple phrases, and mostly kitchen terms.

"Puis-je parler avec Randolph Laurent, s'il vous plaît?" I asked for Randolph with stilted French.

"Juste un momento." The phone clicked as she asked me to wait a moment.

It took almost a full minute before he answered gruffly, "Randolph."

"Bonjour Randolph, c'est Ali. Comment vas-tu?"

"Ah, doux Ali, tout va bien." He paused for one second and then switched to English, for which I was grateful. "I would ask you how you are, but if you are calling me, chérie, something must be wrong."

"Randolph, the health inspector was here today. Someone reported that they ate here last night and came down with E. coli."

"Overnight? Impossible!" he shouted and then started talking in French so fast that there was no chance in hell that I would understand anything. I figured after I heard someone respond to him in the background that he wasn't talking to me. "Did they find anything?"

"No, they did a full inspection and found no signs of the bacteria in our kitchen or our food storage. I agree with you, and I don't think that the man got it from us."

"It was most certainly not! I know your standards and how you run my kitchen. You would not allow such things."

"Thank you, Randolph. Hopefully, it is over, and the report will clear us, but I wanted to make you aware of it."

"Merci mon coeu."

After that, he asked how everything else was going, and we chatted for a few minutes until Ricardo stated that the doors were opening. I excused myself from the call and told him I'd keep him updated.

As I moved into the kitchen, it was all hands on deck. Stocks and soups were on the stove, and pastries were going into the oven. Then I realized that we had done something that we very rarely ever had to do. We pulled out our soup and sauce leftovers from the day before to get us started on the night. Thank god we did this for emergencies such as this. Randolph had said that while he detested leftovers, he would rather have a leftover than nothing to serve.

I walked around the kitchen, checking on things, and then

set my phone up on the stand that I kept it on. When Holly called an hour later, I glanced at it and let it go to voicemail. Now was not the time to think about dates or dancing or television shows. We were having a bustling Wednesday night, and I needed to remain focused.

CHAPTER SEVEN

HARVEY

*S*urprisingly, I was enjoying myself. No, I wasn't a huge fan of dancing, but it was fun to try something new. My sister was off on the side, and she was always smiling when I looked her way. That right there made this whole thing worth the trouble. There wasn't a better feeling in the world than to see her smile.

Maybe it was odd to feel that way about a sister, and perhaps that was because there was no other woman in my life, and no children to focus my attention on. She received all of my affections. I didn't care what other people thought. Holly and I had been close since she was born, and I always felt like I had to watch over her and make sure she was alright.

"So, Harvey, how do you feel about the dance?" Tarin asked as we finished the break and prepared to go through the entire thing one more time.

"To be honest, I feel pretty good. It's been more fun than I anticipated."

"Is there anything that you are getting nervous about?" Tarin asked with a sly smile.

I chuckled. "The whole thing."

"Well, you don't look nervous when you do it. You really did pick it up rather quickly."

I shrugged slightly. "I've never been big on dancing, so I never thought that I would have picked it up so easily."

"After this, are you going to do more dancing?"

I gave her a lopsided grin. "You know, I just might. A friend of mine told me that a way to a girl's heart is to dance with her. So if she picks me, I'll probably be dancing more for sure."

Tarin clapped her hands and giggled. "I love it! Are you worried at all that you might drop her?"

"Honestly, no—okay, maybe a little bit," I replied with a slight chuckle. "I don't think I'll have a problem, but you never know. The last thing I want to do is drop her or miss a step. I just hope that we can flow right through the dance and have a good time."

"And make a connection, right?"

"Well, yeah, of course. That's a given," I replied, and strangely enough, I think I meant it. Somewhere in the last two days, while I'd been making up reasons for being here, I'd started to believe my explanations.

I did want to find a woman to share my life. Was it possible to find one while dancing? Probably—I mean, how many times had I seen a woman from across the room and thought—*her*? There is something about *her*, and then I'd start talking to the woman, and I'd be like yeah—*her*.

That's how it was with both my wives. I hadn't been introduced to them. I'd seen them from across the room. We'd looked at one another; we'd smiled; we'd shared a few flirty glances, and then we'd approached one another, and it went from there. What was so different about dancing?

You were seeing that person for the first time, and you were flirting, and being playful or serious, depending on the dance. Once that was over, she would decide if she wanted to see you again. The only difference was, you didn't get to plead your case or give her a verbal reason to see you again. You had to convince her with your body and your eyes as you moved with hers.

The fact that I was competing with two other men hadn't escaped my mind, and I was all about a little friendly competition.

"What do you want in a woman?" Tarin asked.

That caused me to pause as I thought of an answer. "I want an independent woman, but also one that wants to be part of a couple. I travel quite a bit and work long hours. I need a woman who can accept that schedule and doesn't feel like I'm letting her down."

"Have you had trouble with that in the past?"

I barked out a laugh and glanced toward Holly, who had her hand over her mouth like she couldn't believe that Tarin had just asked me that. "You could say that. A few didn't want to wait around for me to come back. Although back then, I was traveling a lot more than I am now."

"Anything else you'd like to see in a woman?"

"I'd like a woman who doesn't mind me being in the kitchen, because I enjoy cooking, and I want a woman who enjoys food and isn't afraid to laugh or cry around me when she is feeling emotional."

"Wait? Thought all men hated to see a woman cry?"

"Oh, no, I do hate it, but if my woman is going to cry, I want to know why and help her through it."

"I think I just fell a little in love with you," Tarin said sweetly, batting her lashes at me as she put her hand on my arm. "Do you consider yourself a protective man, Harvey?"

"Above and beyond what is normal," I stated, being completely honest. "I'd give my life in a heartbeat to someone I cared for. Hell, I'd do it for a stranger."

"Cut! That's going to be a wrap for today with Harvey," someone called.

Holly came to my side. "I'm so sorry about that."

"It's okay, Holly."

Tarin stepped closer. "Did I say something wrong?"

I shook my head. "No, Holly was worried you'd upset me because my first wife left me while I was on deployment because she didn't like military life, and the second one was in bed with her boss when I came home on leave a couple of days early."

Tarin's jaw dropped. "I'm so sorry, Harvey."

"It's alright, really. It doesn't bother me to talk about it anymore."

"Didn't your last girlfriend have a problem with your travel too?" Holly asked.

"Yeah, she did, but at least we parted amicably."

Tarin put her hand on my shoulder. "Well, maybe you and your date will hit it off, and she will be more independent and not have issues with your traveling."

Holly was gnawing on her bottom lip as I answered Tarin. "Maybe."

Tarin said she'd talk to me later and headed off to get ready for the next guy who was training after me.

Holly accompanied me out of the room. "So, you really do look like you're having fun, Harv."

"Ah, come on, Holly, you know I don't do anything halfway. If I'm going to do it, I might as well have fun and do it right. Besides, maybe it will work out after all."

Holly erupted in a quick burst of laughter. "No offense, Harv, but I told you before, she's not your type."

"Yeah, why do you say that?"

She shook her head and glanced around slightly. "I can't tell you, you know that, but I will tell you that I know her, as a friend, and you are completely not her type. Or she might be your type, but you are not her type."

I laughed. "What type am I?"

"You're tough and controlling, and you expect people to do things your way."

"I do not!" I said.

She threw her head back. "Oh, my god! You most certainly do, Harvey Michael Melton!"

"I don't know what you're talking about, Holly Rose Melton." I chuckled. I knew she was right. I was tough and controlling—not in a bad way though—and yes, I did expect people to do things my way, because that was the right way. However, I would compromise if someone could express valid enough reasons to do so—sometimes.

"Yeah, right! Okay, you need to get out of here; the next guy will be here soon."

"I'm going," I told her. "What time do I show up for dress rehearsal?"

"I'll call you tomorrow with the official time; our female had a little issue at work, and we had to cut her practice short today. I have to nail her down to what time she will be available tomorrow."

"Alright, well, I won't make any plans." I kissed her cheek. "And maybe I'll use the time to figure out what you are going to do for me since I did you this favor."

"No." She laughed. "You said that you were glad you were doing this now. It's no longer a favor."

"Oh, no, this is still a favor. Do you know how many dance memes the guys have sent me because of this?"

She started to walk backward. "Yeah, not my problem that you forgot to remove the eye makeup before you went to work."

"It totally is your problem! You could have reminded me that I had it on."

She smirked. "And where is the fun in that?"

"Yep, see, I always knew you had an evil streak." She laughed. "You up for dinner tonight?"

"No, sorry, things are going to be crazy until Friday night. Maybe this weekend, if you don't have any plans."

"Yeah, I'm sure I can work something out."

I waved goodbye to her and then headed out to the street. I paused a few feet from the door and pulled out my cellphone to send a quick message. As I stood there, another man about my age entered the dance academy door. He was about my height, maybe a bit taller and just as trim, but with short dark-brown hair. I did not doubt that he was one of the other contenders.

It was hard to tell what kind of competition he would be to me, since I couldn't watch him dance, but then again, this wasn't a dance competition. This was about making a connection with the woman. It was about chemistry, and you either had it, or you didn't. None of us would know until we were standing in front of her and looking her in the eye.

It would suck if I felt chemistry with her and then learned that she had felt none for me or had felt more with someone else. It wasn't that I was a sore loser—it was that I didn't like to lose—ever.

I guess in the game of love, you never knew if you were going to be a winner or not. I shook my head as I meandered down the street; so far in life, I hadn't been much of a winner when it came to love. What chance did I have here? Probably not much.

I tried to put the thoughts out of my mind, but they kept creeping back in. By the end of the day, I was literally stressing out about it. It was like I had suddenly become obsessed with this and being the man that she would pick. It didn't make any sense, because there was a fifty-fifty chance that I wouldn't be interested in her.

That brought me up short as I stood in my kitchen and washed dishes. This whole time I'd been worrying about if she would be interested in me. What if I wasn't interested in her and she picked me? Would I be willing to try things out? Would they expect me to do that for the show? I had a feeling that they would expect me to at least meet her if I were the one that she had chosen.

But to be chosen for a real date, I'd have to get selected after Friday's date, and then I'd have to learn a second dance and do it again with her next week.

Would Jake give me the time off? What if he didn't? Luckily, I didn't have anywhere that I needed to travel to, but I did have training classes that I was teaching with Alex and Trevor. Maybe Greg would step in for me and cover. I knew Mike was tied up with all this new website stuff and technology crap that he played with, but Greg had been in hiding for a while, and I bet he would love to get his hands back into training. I'd give him a call tomorrow and ask.

That night as I lay down, my mind ran through all the steps to the dance, and I tried to picture someone else in my arms— other than my current dance partner—but I couldn't. Maybe my mind just wouldn't pull a stranger up and put her in place. For just a brief minute, the face of the woman from the corner popped into my mind as I mentally danced. Then I winced and shifted away from that thought.

Let's just hope that when it was time to dance with someone else, my body responded as well as it did to my current partner.

CHAPTER EIGHT

ALI

I yawned as I got out of my car on the outskirts of the park. It had been an incredibly long night, and I hadn't slept well. The restaurant had been crazy busy for a Wednesday night, and after we'd gotten a late start on everything, we never seemed to be able to catch up entirely until the end of the night. I know that I wasn't the only one that was exhausted, and I'd made sure to thank everyone several times before they left for the night.

It was only nine in the morning when I locked my car door and carried my small bag toward Holly, Cal, and Victor off to the side. There were no live cameras here today, but the film crew was here to oversee and discuss vantage points.

"Morning," I called as I approached the group and then had to stifle a yawn again.

Holly chuckled as she turned to me. "Did you go out partying after work last night? You look like you're dragging."

"Hardly! I am dragging, and I'm sorry for leaving early yesterday, but I had a major problem at the restaurant, and it was a hectic night."

"Everything get straightened out?"

"Yes and no," I replied. "The health inspectors searched our kitchen but couldn't find anything. The guy who got sick swears it was from our place because he's been eating at home for the last two weeks and has eaten the same things as his wife, and she's not sick. They tested her too."

"Oh, no! That's horrible, Ali. What happens now?"

"While they did quick checks for the bacteria, they took a bunch of swabs to have tested at the lab just to confirm. We are waiting for those to come back. If they come back positive, we could be fined or closed. I can't imagine it was from our kitchen, and we are waiting to see if anyone else gets sick. It would be really rare for one person at a restaurant to get sick and no one else."

"Yeah, that doesn't make much sense, does it?"

"No, not really."

"I hope they get it cleared quickly. Are you going to be able to focus on this?"

"Absolutely," I said with more enthusiasm than I felt. "We are so close; I can't give up now. Especially when I am finally starting to gather my courage to do this."

"You're ready to dance with strangers?"

"Ugh, when you put it that way, no!" We all laughed.

Cal threw his arm over my shoulders. "You are going to do fantastic, and I do not doubt that you are going to find love in this. You know, all three of us have bets on who you are going to pick."

"You do?"

"Yep, we sure do, and what's really funny is we all picked someone different, so one of us will be a winner!"

"I guess so."

"Alright, so let's go check out where you'll be dancing, and you and Victor can run through it a few times."

I thought they were going to head toward the park, but they didn't. We ended up crossing the street, which luckily wasn't busy, and Cal walked me through the dance, step by step.

While we would start the dance on this side of the street, we would cross over shortly after it began and move to the gazebo on the other side. A few moments in that area, and then we danced down the stairs to the small fountain, where we'd do the majority of the routine.

The first part of the dance was mostly flirting, coming close, moving away, chasing one another, and coming back together again. Then we'd meet in front of the fountain and dance together as a couple.

It was a beautiful area, and I was excited to try it out officially. When Victor and I took our spots, my stomach began to get all jittery. Tomorrow, I would be doing this three times, with three different men. If I was this nervous now, what was I going to be like tomorrow?

Victor and I started the dance while Tarin held a small music player that was louder than I had expected. They explained that tomorrow, there would be speakers around the area so that the music would travel with us. When it was time to cross the street, we didn't dance, because the road was open now. Instead, we rushed to the other side and went through the moves there before moving on.

The choreography was so perfect that we only had to make one adjustment to the entire routine to make sure that it moved well between the different areas. Tarin and Holly were very pleased, as were the few others that had joined us.

When we got ready to start it again, Cal stood in front of me. "Remember, that you are about to possibly meet the man of your dreams. Let your soul shine as you finally meet his gaze."

"I will!" They started the music again, and we ran through it two more full times before my cellphone wouldn't stop ringing. One of the production assistants brought it to me.

"I'm sorry, but it keeps ringing, and the screen says Ricardo.

After he called the fourth time, I thought maybe it was important enough to bother you with."

"Yes!" I grabbed the phone out of her hands. "Ricardo, what's wrong?"

"Ali, someone else got sick."

"What? No!"

"Unfortunately, yes."

"Is the health department back?"

"Yes, a different team of inspectors, doing a more in-depth inspection. They have already found one issue."

"What issue?"

"You know that tile in front of the freezer that jiggles, they jiggled it enough to make it loose, and it broke. They are hitting us with an unsafe floor."

"But that has absolutely nothing to do with someone getting E. coli!"

"That's what I told them, but they told me to get out of the kitchen while they inspected."

"They kicked you out?" I practically screamed.

"Yes."

"Oh, no, they don't. You march right back in there and watch everything they do. They cannot kick you out! I'm on my way. I'll be there in ten minutes." I hung up without another word, and everyone was staring at me with wide eyes.

"You can't go now; we still need to go over a few things."

"Holly, I'm sorry, but the health department is back in my kitchen, and they are turning everything upside down." I rushed back to the other side of the street to get my stuff, Holly and Tarin in tow. "I'm sorry. I know this messes things up, but I have to be there."

Holly grabbed my arm. "Ali, I know you have to go, I get that, but tell me this: are you going to be able to do this tomorrow? You won't be able to jet out of here if you get another call from work. Ali, I have to remind you that you did sign a contract saying you would do this."

"I know I did, Holly! I promise you that I will be all in tomorrow. I have the night off."

"Just because you have the night off, doesn't mean they can't call you and say help!"

I was torn. My job was everything to me, but I had signed a contract saying I would do this. If I didn't have the contract dangling over my head, I might have told her to forget it. That's how frustrated and stressed I felt at the moment.

I inhaled deeply and released it to try and calm down. "Holly, I know that I signed a contract, and I know that a lot of people are counting on me, but right now, more people are counting on me in my kitchen. Their jobs are at stake, their livelihoods, and our reputation. This isn't just a silly date; it's about my career and other people's lives. I'm sorry, Holly, I have to go. I'll call you later."

"Alright," she said uneasily.

I dashed off and back to my car. I was there in twelve minutes and pulled my car down the alley toward the restaurant. The whole way there, I tried not to dwell over the way I'd taken off. I felt terrible for what I'd said to Holly. I knew that I'd hurt her when I'd called the whole thing silly, but in comparison to what was going on, it was. I understood that this was her job, and she was trying to do it to the best of her ability. This was *my* job, and I owed it to my employees and the owner of the restaurant to do everything I could.

There were two parking spots in the alley behind the restaurant, one for me and one for Randolph, or the manager, Anton, when Randolph was not around. Ricardo and Anton were leaning against Anton's car.

"They kicked you out again?"

"Yeah, they didn't want anyone in there."

"Yeah, well, they can't kick me out. It's my kitchen!" I

growled toward them as I made a beeline toward the back door. I yanked the door open and stepped into the back. There were two inspectors in the kitchen, both wearing face masks and gloves, and they turned to me when I stepped through the kitchen archway.

"You can't be in here," one man said.

"I most certainly can. I'm Ali Davidson, the Head Chef of this kitchen, and I oversee everything when Randolph is not around."

"Where is the owner?"

"Randolph is currently in France."

"Is he aware that your kitchen is precariously close to being permanently closed?"

"I don't know how you can say that. There was one person who was reported to be sick with E. coli, and that was less than fourteen hours after he ate here. I'm sure you are aware of the incubation period, so I seriously question that this person might have contracted that from this kitchen."

"It's not unheard of for a person to get sick in less than twenty-four hours," the gruff man said. He had yet to identify himself to me either.

"You need to go back outside and wait until we are done."

"I most certainly will not!" I crossed my arms and glared at him. "This is my kitchen, and I will remain in it. I will stay out of your way, but I have every right to be here and oversee what you are doing. You cannot bully my staff or me, and you can start by identifying yourself to me and supplying me with a copy of the second complaint."

I could only see part of the man's face, but I could tell he was livid at my refusal and at my demand to have information. As he stormed off to the side, I glanced at the other man, and he winked at me. I frowned as I turned away. Was he flirting—or telling me that he approved of my outburst?

It didn't matter one way or the other. The angry man came

back and thrust a paper at me along with a business card. He glared at me, then spun around and strode off to get back to work.

I read the report. A female who had been in our restaurant the same night as the man had reported feeling sick and had gone to the hospital after intense stomach and bowel issues. She was confirmed to have E. coli in her system. I closed my eyes briefly and breathed slowly.

I moved down further on the report and saw that she had skipped the salad, eaten the fish, and had crème brûlée for dessert. Nothing that the other man had eaten, and from different stations altogether! This made no sense.

Fish was stored differently than our other meat, the vegetables prepared and cooked separately, and the dessert finished in a different area than the crepes. How were these people getting sick? Was it possible that we did have a more significant issue in our kitchen?

The paper dropped to my side as I scanned the room; where were the bacteria, and how many other people had we gotten sick?

For two hours, Henry Marks and his assistant, Carl, worked the room, searching and testing every surface, wall, floor, counter, and stove. They even got on a ladder and took samples of the ceiling and air vents. I was glancing at my watch, noting that the rest of the employees would start arriving soon.

"If you're worried about the time, Ms. Davidson, don't be. Your restaurant will be closed until we get these samples tested."

"What? But you haven't even had any positive tests in the swabs you have done!"

"Yes, that's true, but with two people having such a severe reaction, and the fact that we can't pinpoint where or how, until we get the swabs back, your doors will be closed."

"You can't do that!" I spouted angrily, and he turned, pulling his mask down and smiling at me.

"Actually, I can. I have every right to do that, and as soon as I sign my report, it will be official. So call all your employees and tell them not to report to work. No one other than you, the manager, and the sous chef are allowed in here until we get this figured out."

"You're kidding me? I can't even have the staff come in for a special cleansing?"

"Nope, not until we figure out where it is coming from. Nothing can be added or removed until then."

"Not even dry pantry goods? We have a major delivery tomorrow."

He inhaled deeply, and then released it in a huff. "Normally, I'd say no, but your pantry storage is very separate and well contained. I can't imagine that is where the bacteria is coming from. I'll let you take the delivery tomorrow, but again, only the three of you may accept the inventory and put it in storage. No one should be in the kitchen working with any tools or food, and no other deliveries."

"How long do you think we'll be closed?"

"Well, it's Thursday, so the samples won't be there until tomorrow. I'm going to say probably at least until Saturday, but it could be Monday."

"Monday?" I squeaked.

CHAPTER NINE

HARVEY

Thursday afternoon was a little intense. I met them at the location, and we ran through the dance four times. I struggled the first two times, feeling uncomfortable being out in public and dancing.

Holly had pulled me aside after the second one. "Harvey, since when have you ever cared what people think of you?"

"What are you talking about?"

"I'm talking about the fact that you are distracted, and you keep looking around. It's obvious that you aren't comfortable doing this in front of others."

"You are one hundred percent right; I am not."

"Forget they are there. They mean nothing, Harvey. The only person who means anything is your partner. You can do this, but you need to forget about the audience and get your head on straight."

"You're right, Holly." I was stuck in the fact that people were watching us practice. Had we been doing tactical things, I wouldn't have cared because I was comfortable with it—but this was dancing. Over the last few days, I'd had a handful of people who had been present during the practices while they recorded everything. I just had to pretend that those other people here now were just like them. They were doing a job, not judging me.

Holy shit, I was going to dance in public with someone I didn't even know! A panic I hadn't ever felt before gripped my gut for a second. Get it together, Harv! You got this. You got this.

A few minutes later, I had things back under control, and we ran through the dance two more times. Both of them were flawless, or, well, as flawless as they were going to be with me doing them.

Now I just needed to make it through the next day and do it for real. As I left the park, I wondered if I was more nervous about messing up or having a connection with the woman and never seeing her again.

Friday morning, I woke up feeling even more anxious than the day before. As the day progressed, I began to feel downright nervous. I tried everything to keep from thinking about it, but the closer it got to noon, the twitchier I became.

I realized that I wasn't as nervous about meeting her, as I was nervous about doing the dance and messing up. I didn't want to embarrass myself or her, and I knew that if I screwed up during the dance, my guys would never let me live it down. Even five days later, I was still getting texts of funny memes and videos of guys dancing and making total fools of themselves. I knew it was in jest, but I couldn't afford to add to the fire.

I wasn't sure how they pulled it off, but Alice and Maggie were going to be there to watch from behind the scenes. I hadn't wanted anyone there, but Alice told me last night that they would be. I wondered if maybe Maggie had used her newspaper credentials to get her a place.

At noon, I headed down to my staging area and checked in. I was brought to a small trailer and asked to wait there. I could hear people walking by outside, talking about camera angles and sound checks, and I thought I would explode out of my skin if I had to wait any longer in this closet. I was ready to start pacing, and I never paced.

Finally, the door opened, and Holly stepped in. "Hey! Are you ready for this?" She gave me a wide grin as she approached, her arms open wide.

"Ready as I'll ever be." I held her close.

"How are you feeling?"

"Strangely anxious." I laughed slightly.

"That's normal. Once you start dancing, that will go away."

"Yeah, but what if I screw up?"

"Then you screw up, and you move on."

"What if there is no connection?"

She frowned. "Harvey, I talked you into doing this because I needed a favor. I never expected you to have chemistry with her, and I never for the life of me thought that you might want to have a connection with her."

I shrugged. "Well, you know that I never do anything halfway."

"Yes, I know, but don't be too disappointed if she doesn't pick you. I'm serious about you not being her type. You're like a wolf, and she's a church mouse."

I snickered at her analogy. "Don't worry, I won't be upset, but I guess I was thinking that it might be kind of cool to hit it off with someone while doing this. It's not all that different than being in a bar and seeing someone from across the room."

"No, it's not. The only difference is you don't talk." She studied me. "You know if she doesn't pick you, and you're still interested in this whole process, I might be able to get you on again with us picking three women for you. Might be better odds for you."

I laughed loudly. "Hey, let's not go overboard. Let me get through today before you start trying your matchmaking skills on me, alright?"

"Alright, fine. I came in here to check on you, but also to tell you that you are going to be first today."

"Will I be able to watch the other two men dance with her?"

"Nope."

"Seriously? I won't even be able to see how she connects with them?"

She shook her head. "Nope. You won't see anything until it airs."

"When is that?"

"In about two months, after this whole decision is made and then it goes through editing."

"You know, it's amazing that you film everything for two weeks, and it breaks down to less than sixty minutes of tape."

"I know. We work hard to pull out the perfect snippets for the show. It takes hours to do."

"I do not doubt that it does. So what time is my dance?"

She glanced at her watch. "At two. So we need to get you to makeup and wardrobe."

"Lead the way," I told her and followed her from the trailer. There was a lot of activity around, and I saw the man from the other day being led to another nearby trailer. He nodded to me after he'd looked me over from head to toe. What did he think of his competition?

Holly brought me to another trailer, larger than the first, and inside I was introduced to a different makeup and hair lady, Gina, and the wardrobe guy, Stu.

It didn't take me long to get made up, and there wasn't much she could do with my hair, not with the way I had it cut. I was wearing jeans, sneakers, and a light-purple button-down shirt. I'd never worn purple before in my life, but I liked it as I stared at the reflection in front of me. It brought out my eyes, but then again, that could be the makeup that was bringing out my eyes.

One of the production staff walked me back to the trailer and told me to hang tight for about fifteen minutes. After that, someone would come to get me, and I could stretch out and get ready. The minute the door closed, my stomach rolled. Holy crap, I'd never been this nervous in my life. Not even going into military operations. I'd gone into some pretty scary places, but this seemed ten times worse.

It didn't make sense. It totally did not make sense. I should be laughing this off, making fun of myself, but I couldn't. All I could do was wonder who she was, what she would look like, and if there would be any chemistry between us.

I know that Holly said there was no chance in hell, but crazier things had happened in life. I think the wildest part of the whole thing was that I wanted crazy to happen. Maybe I'd lost my mind.

To take my mind off the questions, I stood and began to walk through certain parts of the dance in the small space that I had. My cellphone beeped, and I checked it to see Alice sending me a message saying they were there and so excited. She wished me well and told me not to break my leg.

I told her thank you for coming and then turned off my phone. I didn't want any more distractions.

A few minutes later, a young guy came to get me. He brought me in front of a camera crew, and Tarin joined me. "Are you nervous, Harvey?"

"I'd be lying if I said no."

"How do you feel?"

To be honest, my fingers were tingling, and my stomach was a mess, but I wasn't going to say that. "I'm excited and ready to meet her—and okay, more nervous than I have ever been."

"Are you still hoping for a connection with her when you do?"

"Yes, even more so now than before."

Tarin cocked her head. "Why is that?"

I shrugged slightly and laughed. "I don't know. I guess when I started this, I wasn't one hundred percent invested in it or the idea, but now I am. Now I'm really excited to dance with her, and while we aren't going to be talking, I hope that our bodies say all they need to."

"Cut!" the director said, and Tarin leaned toward me. "I have a feeling your bodies are going to be doing a lot of talking."

"Let's hope so."

Holly approached me. "Alright, it's almost time. Go with Cal; he's going to get you over there, and Ryan is going to let you know when you can take your place. As soon as you are both in place, we will start the music, and the stage will be yours."

I noticed a camera over her shoulder on me, and I nodded and tried to smile. The butterfly in my stomach had turned into a full-sized bird. Now it was banging around in my stomach so hard I was expecting it to burst out at any moment.

"You ready?"

"As I'll ever be." She hugged me, and I whispered into her ear. "How did I let you talk me into this?"

She laughed as she leaned back. "You love me, that's how! Now, go show her your stuff."

I headed with Cal and Ryan across the street and down the side street slightly. The main road was now closed, but there was an area for spectators, plus a lot of production crew and cameras.

Holy shit! What the hell was I doing? I bent over at the waist, putting my hands on my knees, and tried to calm myself. I seriously had never been so nervous in my life. Why? I was only going to dance with a woman. I'd danced with women before, dozens of them, so why was this such a big deal?

It has to be because of the cameras; that was the only thing I could think of or the fact that I wouldn't say a word to this woman for the four minutes we were together.

"You ready?" Ryan asked.

"Yeah, let's go." I stood and inhaled a few times deeply as I tried to center myself. Pretend you are going into a battle zone;

people depend on you; it's a dangerous place, and you need to keep your head on a swivel and focus. I could do this.

"Get ready, when I drop my hand, you start walking toward the corner and get yourself ready. She is already going to be there."

I nodded, and a few seconds later, he dropped his hand, and it was showtime. As I approached my spot, I tried to remember the dance, but it was hiding under my anxiety. As I reached my place, I saw her knee on the other side of the corner, and I smiled. Holy shit, I was actually going to do this.

I leaned back against the wall, inhaled slowly, and felt the calm descend. We would either have a connection or we wouldn't. Either way, we were going to have fun.

The music began, and just like that, the dance came back to me as I leaned sideways and peered around the corner. Her dark hair was pulled up in a ponytail, and she wore matching sneakers to mine, jean shorts, and a darker purple shirt. I saw all of this in one single peek before I pulled back and turned my head away.

I waited for the beat and put my hand out; a moment later, her small hand landed in mine. It was almost electrifying, and I stepped out and pulled her into me. My hand skimmed down her side to where I took her hand, and I grinned as I twirled her away from me and then pulled her back.

This time as she returned, her face snapped to mine, and her hand came to rest on my cheek. The cameras did not exist. The spectators weren't there. Hell, in that single moment, the entire world vanished as I stared down into her energetic green eyes.

It wasn't until she pulled away from me with a sassy grin on her face that I realized I'd seen this woman before, but I didn't have time to think on it as we danced and moved over the street, onto the gazebo, and then down the stairs to the fountain.

The entire way, I grinned like a freaking fool. I couldn't have stopped if I had wanted to. Every time she looked at me, I felt it shoot straight down my spine. I picked her up, spun her around, heard her giggle, and then put her down on the fountain wall. She did a little dance, wagged her finger at me with the sexiest smile I'd ever seen, and then I was there, lifting her into the air.

She was light as a feather, and the only thing I wanted to do was bring her down to my body and hold her close. I wanted to stare into her eyes, suck in her breath, and learn everything about who she was.

The dance went too fast, and before I knew it, she was wrapped in my arms for the final note of the song. Both of us were breathing hard, and neither of us moved away from the other. It was like time stopped again, and nothing else existed. I ran two fingers down the side of her face, and we slowly parted. The two of us stepped apart, and it was almost painful to turn. I held eye contact with her until the very last moment, and then we were walking away from one another. I glanced back; I couldn't help it, and she did too, her bottom lip tucked under her teeth before she made the turn out of sight.

The smile was still on my face as I came around a bunch of trees, and the camera crew was standing there; a whiteboard faced me off-camera with the question, "How do you feel?"

"Holy crap," I said as I stood there trying to slow my breathing. "My heart is going a million miles an hour. That was crazy. I'm just—I'm just—um—I'm kind of speechless. That was fantastic; she is fantastic."

CHAPTER TEN

ALI

"What just happened?" I said as I stopped in front of the camera. My heart was beating so fast and hard in my chest that I couldn't hear. "Seriously, what just happened?"

I glanced over my shoulder, but of course, there was nothing to see. The man that I had just danced with was gone.

Tarin came to my side, her smile slightly nervous. "Well, was it good?"

"Oh, my god! It was incredible. He was so handsome, and the moment I looked into his eyes, I was immediately comfortable. It was like I knew that we were going to have fun, and he was going to lead me through it, and he wouldn't drop me."

"So, you weren't worried anymore about him dropping you?"

"No, not at all."

"Would you say you felt a connection?"

I nodded like a bobblehead doll. "Oh, yes, I felt a connection. It was crazy, but I felt it."

Tarin laughed. "It was obvious as we watched that you two had a bond from the very first moment. The look on his face when he stared down at you was like he was surprised to see it was you. Like he had expected someone else."

"I felt the same way; I felt like I knew the man the moment we locked eyes."

"Well, let's hope that your next two dances are just as good, or not." She laughed, and my eyes went huge. "Now, you need to clear your head, forget about that dance, and do it again."

"I can't believe I have to do that two more times."

The director cut after that, and I was moved swiftly away from the area to change clothes and touch up my makeup. I was given a bottle of water and asked if I wanted a snack, but there was no way I could eat anything.

The entire time I got ready for the next dance, my mind was on the first one. When I had peeked around the corner and seen how tall he was, his dark hair, the way he was dressed, my heart sighed. Then I had taken his hand, and it was warm and slightly rough, and it thrilled me, but not as much as him twirling me into his arms and running his nose up the side of my head as his fingers ran down the side of my body—my god that was so damn sexy.

Then I was looking in his eyes, and I wanted to fall. I wanted just to jump in and get lost in his deep green gaze. As I started to turn away from him, I realized that I had seen him before. On the street corner during the downpour, almost exactly like this, and he had picked up my bags and handed them to me before he had rushed off. That night, he had looked stressed, worried, but not tonight. Tonight, he was confident, playful, and so damn sexy!

The dance had been so much fun, and even though I didn't know the man, I couldn't imagine doing this dance with anyone else. What was it going to be like to do it again with two more men? Holy crap, what if I had connections with all three men?

It was thirty minutes later, and I was retaking my place. This time I wasn't as nervous, but my heart was still racing. When the music started, and I peered around the corner, the guy was taller, and his hair was a lighter shade of brown. When I came face-to-face with him, I smiled brightly. He was super cute, and he even had a dimple in his cheek.

The dance was fun, and I had a good time, but I didn't feel the same connection with him that I had with the first man. When he lifted me into the air, I felt him shift slightly, and for a second, I thought he might drop me. The first man would never have dropped me. If I were going to fall, he probably would have thrown his body under mine to soften the blow—how I knew that I wasn't sure—I just did.

As the dance ended, we shared another energetic smile, and I turned from his arms and strolled away at a fast pace. He had a sweet smile, kind eyes, and he seemed very fun, but nothing urged me to look back as I had the last time.

"That was so much fun!" I said as I reached the camera crew. I knew they wanted my first reaction, and that was the truth. It was fun.

Tarin stepped up and hugged me. "It looks like you two were having a blast."

"We were! I really felt like we connected on a different level. I wanted to throw my head back and laugh; he had a playful vibe to him."

"Did you feel a connection with him?"

"Yes, I did, very different than the first one."

"It makes you think, doesn't it?"

I nodded. "It does. I'm going to have to figure out if I want serious or playful because that's kind of what I felt between the two of them. One was more intense, the other very playful."

"Yes, I got that too, but before you decide, you have another dance to get ready for."

"Oh, my gosh! One more time! This is going to make it so hard. If the third guy is half as good as these two were, I'm not sure what I will do."

I played to the camera a little bit because I was pretty sure that if the decision was between the first or second, it would be the first guy. Not that I didn't want someone playful. I did want to have fun, but where the second guy was sweet and cute, the first one was sexy and powerful. Right now, where I was in life, I think I was more interested in power and sex than someone who just wanted to have fun.

I got ready for the third dance, and this time, I asked for a little snack while I was getting touched up. They brought me some cut fruit, and it was enough to satisfy me for the moment.

Right before I went on for my third dance, Holly approached me. "How are you holding up? Are you having fun?"

I hugged her. "I'm having so much fun, and I'm tired, but the adrenaline is keeping me up and moving."

"You are doing fantastic." She glanced around and lowered her voice. "Between friends, which one did you like better, the first one or second one?"

I peered around quickly. "The first one."

Holly's grinned exploded over her face. "I knew it!"

"Wait? Is that the one you picked?"

"I can't tell you that, and you still have one more to dance with."

"Yes, I do. What did you think of the dances?"

"Let's just say that you look like you are having so much fun, and so do they."

"Do you know what they've said when they were done?"

"I can't tell you that!" Holly said with a laugh. "But I will tell you that they both had a great time and were all smiles. Now, you go, do your last dance so we can talk."

"Sounds good."

A few minutes later, the music started, and we were off for the final time. He had large hands, and he was much taller than the last two men, with blond hair and bright-blue eyes.

The dance went smoothly, and every time we came eye to

eye, my heart raced a little faster. If it kept up, my heart was going to wear itself out. He had no issues with lifting me over his head, and as I stared at him at the end, I found myself enjoying his smile and the way he was looking at me. We stayed together for an extra second or two, and then slowly split apart. I glanced back at him, but he was already turning the corner.

"Holy smokes!" I said as I reached the camera area. "That was —holy smokes!"

Tarin joined me. "That was a great dance! It looked like you two really connected out there."

"I think we did. I was having so much fun just looking into his eyes, and he kind of made my heart beat a little faster."

"Boy, do you have a tough decision to make."

"You aren't kidding!" I said. "I have no idea what I'm going to do."

"Well, the good news is that you don't have to decide tonight. You can think it over and make a decision tomorrow."

"Tomorrow? I'm not sure I'm going to have enough time to decide."

"I'm sure you'll figure it out," Tarin said, and the director yelled that's a wrap for the day.

I glanced around as everyone started to move at once. For the last four hours, I'd been running at super speed; now it was done, and I wasn't sure what to do with myself. The first thing was to find my cellphone and see if anything had been found out about the restaurant.

Holly grabbed my arm right before I went into the trailer I was using. "You did fantastic. You looked like you were really enjoying that last dance."

"I was, he was great. I felt like I had a connection with him too."

"So, are you going to pick one or three?"

"I'm not sure. I need to think about it for a while." We stepped inside, and I went straight for my phone. After turning it back on, I shifted to face her. "I owe you an apology for the way I acted yesterday."

"No, you don't. I understand that you are dealing with a lot. You were right; this is a dance show, and it's just a few dates, and the problem you are dealing with is making people sick, and all those employees. I get it. I was wrong to attack you like that yesterday."

I hugged her. "Thank you for understanding, Holly, I appreciate it."

"You got it, and to show you how much I understand it, how about we go grab some dinner?"

"Let me check my phone and see if anything has come up." I checked messages, but there was nothing and no texts. "Looks like dinner would be perfect."

"I have a few things that I need to do, but I'll be ready in about twenty minutes."

"I can wait for you."

"Great, hey, do you mind if a friend of mine joins us?"

"No, not at all."

"Fantastic. I'll find her and let her know."

Holly took off, and I changed into my own clothing, setting aside the three outfits that I'd worn today. All similar, but different, except the shoes. The shoes had been the same white sneakers in all three dances.

I was going to take the makeup off, but it still looked good, so I kept it on. I was wandering around, looking for Holly, when I saw two women talking to a man in the distance. From the back, it looked like the first man I had danced with, although he was wearing khaki pants and a black polo shirt. I slipped out of sight and watched them, trying to get more information on him.

Holly joined them, and they were all laughing and smiling for a moment before he kissed two of them on the cheek and then hugged Holly tightly. He turned and glanced back, but I was completely hidden in the shadows. He looked relaxed and handsome, and I was tempted to make myself visible to see what he would do. However, we weren't supposed to talk to one another—at all.

He walked away, and the three women started coming my way. I stepped out from behind a bush, not wanting them to know I saw them. "Hey, Holly, are you ready?"

The two women with her looked me up and down and then turned to Holly.

"Yep, I sure am. We were just coming to get you. Ali, this is Alice, and this is Maggie."

I wanted to ask them how they knew the first dancer, but I kept my mouth shut and smiled as Maggie spoke up. "I did an article on Holly and the show when she first started this."

"Wait! You're Maggie Valor! I recognize you now. You write the romance column."

"I did," Maggie said quickly with a chuckle. "I recently left and got a new job."

"I loved your column; your replacement is horrible."

The four of us headed toward the parking lot while we discussed her column and replacement. All thoughts of dancer one, two, and three were put on the shelf so I could unwind for a few minutes and enjoy myself with Holly and her friends.

CHAPTER ELEVEN

HARVEY

I couldn't stop thinking about it—or more importantly—her. I couldn't believe that we had literally run into each other on the street a week ago. I wasn't going to mention that, and no one said anything to me, so I assumed she hadn't spoken about it either—or perhaps she didn't remember me.

I'm pretty sure she did. I saw a moment of recognition before we moved along. I tried to think back on that night, and what she could have thought of me. The words we spoke were few, and I tried to recall the sound of her voice, but I'd been so distracted that I hadn't taken the time to pop it into my memory banks. I'd merely collected her bags and walked away.

I guess it didn't matter if she remembered me or not, or what she had said that night. The more important question right now was, would she want a second dance?

I was pretty sure she had enjoyed herself while we were dancing. Otherwise, once we'd finished, she wouldn't have hesitated for so long. As if she didn't want to leave me. I'd felt it. I'd been tempted to wrap her in my arms, maybe press my lips to hers. The thought to pick her up and swing her around again had crossed my mind. What if I had run away with her? How far would we have gotten before we came to our senses?

I was dying to know how her other two dances went, but no one would tell me anything, including my sister, and it frustrated the hell out of me.

It was funny how patient I could be sitting behind a gun, but waiting to find out if the woman had been interested in me, well, that was going to drive me nuts.

I was pulling into my driveway when I got a call. I glanced at my phone and immediately picked it up. "Did you hear anything?"

There was a long pause. "Hear anything about what?" Greg asked.

Uh, why did I even think he would know? Maybe because I had expected Maggie to tell him about how it had gone and if I had made a fool out of myself. Had she said something to the effect, he would have started the conversation out that way. I shook my head. "Nothing, what's up?"

"You busy tonight? Maggie went out to dinner with some friends. Thought maybe you might want to grab a bite."

"That sounds like a great idea. I'm just getting home; let me shower and change. I need to make sure all the makeup is off."

He chuckled. "That's right. You had your dance date thingy today. How did that go?"

"I'll tell you about it over a drink."

"Sounds good. Meet me at the pub on Tenth."

"You got it."

It didn't take me long to shower and get dressed, and I was at the pub forty-five minutes later. Greg was already at the bar, and I took the stool beside him as I slapped his back.

"How was work this week?"

"Damn, man, it's good to be back. Don't get me wrong, it was nice having Maggie all to myself for weeks on end, but I was starting to go nuts at the cabin."

"Weren't you working at all?"

"I was, I mean, I was doing some research and working on a few different ideas for some training, but I was ready to come home. That place was getting too small."

I chuckled. "So are you back at your place now?" I asked after the bartender took my order.

Greg grinned at me. "No. I'm still at Maggie's. It's a bigger place; we aren't on top of each other there."

"How is it working together? That's not too much time together, living and working together, is it?"

His brow lined for a second. "You know, I hadn't even thought about that until you said something, but no. I don't mind working with Maggie or living with her. Maggie does her own thing; she's probably the most independent woman that I know—well, except Alice." We both laughed. "In fact, I barely saw Mags all week at work. She spent more time with Mike and Jake than me." He grinned at me before he took a sip of his beer.

"That's good. Says a lot about her if she can put up with you being around all the time."

He snickered. "Yeah, she is probably getting the raw end of the deal."

"Oh, of that I have no doubt."

"Where is she tonight?"

"She went out to dinner with a few friends." He smirked as he picked up his phone, pushed a few things on the screen, then spun through some images. He handed me the phone, and my jaw dropped.

In the picture were Alice, Holly, and my dance partner. "She's out with my sister."

"Yep, and your date. She's pretty hot, by the way. How did it go? Mags said you did a surprisingly good job. She hadn't pictured you to be able to dance."

"What else did she say?" I stared at the picture, but I was zeroed in on the woman. "What is her name?"

"I have no idea, and she didn't say anything else. She specifically told me she wasn't saying anything so that I couldn't tell you when you asked."

I checked the post, and it only said, *Girls night with friends.* "Seriously? She didn't say anything else?"

"She said the chemistry between the two of you was snapping off the monitor, whatever the hell that means."

I grinned. "That means that we were good together."

He laughed. "You enjoyed yourself, didn't you?"

"I did. I never expected to, but I did enjoy doing it."

He asked me how I had gotten involved in it in the first place, and I told him the story. When I finished, he asked, "When do you see her again?"

I shrugged. "I have no clue if I will."

He frowned. "What do you mean?"

"It's up to her if she wants a second date. If she does, then I find out tomorrow, and I learn another dance, and we do it again. Then she decides if she wants to meet me and speak to me face-to-face."

He barked out a laugh. "You haven't even spoken to this woman?"

"Nope." I took a long draw off my beer. "When the music started, I put my hand out, she took it, we danced for about four minutes, then we turned and walked away from each other."

"That's nuts, man."

"When you think about it, it is, but it's kinda cool, too. I mean, I never would have signed up to do something like this on my own. If it hadn't been for Holly needing someone to fill in, I wouldn't be doing it this time."

"Do you think she will pick you?"

"Maybe, although I don't know how her other two dances went. Maybe she connected with one of them more than me."

He smirked at me. "You want to get picked, don't you?"

"It's crazy, but I do. When Holly first talked me into this, it was the furthest thing from my mind, but then I started enjoying myself and thought this could be something pretty cool to tell my kids one day."

He laughed. "Jesus, you've danced with her once, and you're having kids? You've lost your fucking mind."

I snickered and sipped from my bottle. "What about you and Maggie? You think you guys are going to get married, have a kid or two?"

"No kids. I'm pretty sure eventually we'll tie the knot, but no kids for us."

"You don't want any?"

"No, I don't, and," he paused, tapped his thumb on the bar for a moment as if he were making a decision, and turned to me, "and Maggie can't have kids. Don't tell anyone about that, though."

"Oh, man, I'm sorry to hear that. Did she want kids? You guys could always adopt."

"She's not interested in kids. She'd prefer to travel and work. She's not a very maternal person, except when she's taking care of her mom."

"How is her mom doing?"

"Eh, she has her days. She recognized us when we first came back, but once in a while, she won't know us. I gotta tell you, Maggie does better with it than I do."

"She's had more time to get used to it."

"Do you ever get used to the fact that your parent doesn't recognize you?"

"Okay, so maybe not. That sucks."

"Yeah, it does, but Maggie rolls with it. Sometimes she gets a little sad, but she deals with it pretty well."

"She's a pretty awesome woman. I look forward to getting to know her better."

"Yeah, well, if things work out for you with this dancing girl, maybe we can have you all over for dinner."

"Let's see what tomorrow brings."

After that, Greg and I turned the conversation over to work and moved to a table to eat. I didn't think about the illustrious dancer again until I was crawling in bed.

As I closed my eyes, her bright-green eyes carried me toward my dreams, and the memory of the feel of her body made me wish she were here with me. Maybe I was turning into a sap in my old age.

* * *

THE NEXT MORNING, I dressed and headed down to the dance studio at my appointed time. It was time to find out if I had made the next round.

As soon as I entered, I was whisked away to one of the rooms to do makeup, and then they started recording right from the front door as if I had just come in.

Tarin hugged me on camera. "Did you enjoy yourself yesterday?"

"I did."

"What was your favorite part?"

"Looking into her eyes and seeing her smile up at me."

"Did you feel like you connected with her?"

"Surprisingly, I did. I didn't expect that, but the minute I looked down at her, I felt a spark."

"Well, are you ready to find out if she felt the same way?"

"I am."

"Alright, head up the stairs, and at the top, there will be three boxes. Your box is number one. I can't wait to see if you have an invitation to come back."

"Okay, let's check it out," I said, and as I started to climb the stairs, a camera crew in front of me, I tried not to let my nerves show. At the top was a long table with three white boxes, each one labeled with a number. I went straight to one and paused as I stared down at it. Oh, please let it be an invite to come back.

I lifted the box and found an envelope under it. I set the box down and picked up the envelope, turning it over to open the flap and remove the card inside. I grinned and read the card out loud. "May I have the next dance?"

I grinned so widely that my cheeks hurt as I turned toward the camera. "Looks like she felt it too!" I held the card up for the camera to see.

As I took the steps down, I practically skipped, and Tarin met me at the bottom of the stairs. "Good news?"

I held the card up. "Looks like I have a hot date next Friday!"

"That's great! We will see you on Monday to start working on your other routine."

"I'm looking forward to it." The cameras cut off, and I found Holly standing off to the side, grinning. I sauntered off toward her. "What are you grinning at?"

"You. I haven't seen you smile this much in a very long time." She giggled.

"Whatever, did you all have fun last night?"

She cocked her head to the side. "What are you talking about?"

"I know you went out to dinner with Maggie, Alice, and my date. Did you all have fun?"

"How do you know that?"

"I was out with Greg; he showed me a picture of you all out having fun." She narrowed her eyes, and I held my hand up. "Before you lose your shit, I don't know anything else about her —not even her name. It was just a picture around a table. I didn't even know what she was drinking, and I didn't try to stalk her to learn more." She looked unconvinced. "Trust me, Holly. I'm enjoying the mystery, although if you want to tell me anything about her, I'd be happy to listen."

"No, and you need to leave, the second guy is on his way in."

"Do you know if he got picked?"

"I can't tell you that."

"Oh, come on." I paused. "Did you think she would pick me?"

Her face went completely blank. "No. I told you I thought you weren't her type."

"See how wrong you were!"

"Yeah, well, let's see what this week brings you." She walked me to the door. "Do you think Jake will give you a hard time about work?"

"Nah, I found someone to cover for me if I did get picked."

"Alright, then we will see you on Monday." She hugged me and then leaned back. "Thanks for doing this, Harv."

I kissed her cheek. "You know I'd do anything for you, Holly."

"Yeah, well, when it comes to love, you don't always listen."

I laughed as I stepped back toward the door. "Because the last person I want to take love advice from is my baby sister."

"And look at how right I was about this."

I paused. "I thought you said I wasn't her type." Again, her face went devoid of any emotion.

"You're not."

I smirked her way. "You are a terrible liar, Holly. But that's good to know. I'll see you on Monday, kiddo."

As I stepped away, I grinned. Maybe it was time to listen to my sister, after all.

CHAPTER TWELVE

ALI

*I*t was fun to be out with friends. Even though I didn't know Alice or Maggie, I felt like I did. There was a ton of laughter and a few jokes that went over my head about a guy named Jake. All of those seemed to be targeted toward Alice.

"Is Jake your boyfriend?" I asked after the third one volleyed over the table.

Alice looked horrified. "No! He's my boss."

Maggie snickered. "Yeah, but she wants to sleep with him."

"I do not!" Alice said indignantly.

"Oh, please!" Holly cried. "I'm barely around you two, and I know you want to sleep with him."

Alice turned wide eyes toward her. "How can you say that? He is the crudest, most ignorant, narcissistic man that I have ever met."

"And sexy as hell," Maggie tacked on. "Although not as sexy as Greg or Har—" Maggie's eyes darted to mine and then jumped away. "I'm just saying all the men are sexy; even if Jake is an ass, he'd probably be amazing in bed."

Was it me, or did Alice and Holly also tense when Maggie

started to mention this other man? Was it Harry? Harmon? Hardy? I didn't get much of a chance to think it over as they began discussing Jake in detail.

"Do you two work together?" I asked Alice and Maggie.

"Yep, we do. I just started there as the media liaison," Maggie stated proudly. "That's why I left the paper."

"What kind of company is it?" I asked.

"Tactical security company," Alice answered and glanced at Holly, who seemed tense. "And no fun to talk about, trust me. So tell us, what did you really think of those guys tonight?"

Maggie jumped right on that. "Did you feel sparks with all of them?"

Holly seemed to relax and even smiled as she turned to study me. Whatever was making her tense had instantly vanished.

"Well, I guess I felt something with all of them, although the second one I danced with was more of a friendship feeling." I glanced around the group and let my gaze land on Holly. "Am I allowed to talk about this with them?"

Holly put her hand over my wrist. "Do you know who you are going to pick?"

I nodded. "Yeah, I think so."

Holly nodded. "You can talk about it with us, but not with anyone else. I trust these two not to say anything." She gave them very pointed looks. "We would never want to sway your decision."

"Okay, well, the first guy was very handsome and sexy in a tough and stormy kind of way, and yeah, I felt sparks with him, but I was so nervous that I don't know if they were romantic sparks or fear tremors." I laughed nervously as Maggie and Alice glanced at each other. They knew guy number one; were they rooting for him? Of course, they were! "I wasn't as nervous the second and third time, so I'm still wondering if what I felt for the first one was real or not."

"What did you think of the second guy?" Maggie asked.

"He was cute too, but I got more of a friend vibe from him. Does that make sense?"

Alice nodded. "Of course, it makes sense."

"I thought for a moment that he was going to drop me during the lift, but then he righted himself, and the rest of the dance went smoothly."

"What about the third dancer?" Holly queried.

"Oh, he was very handsome, and I definitely felt a spark with him. He made me feel safe, too. Maybe it was because he was so big, but he did. However, the first guy made me feel safe also."

Alice asked with a raised brow, "How did he make you feel safe?"

I shook my head and shrugged. "I don't know. There was just something about him. Although I don't need a man to feel safe."

"None of us need a man to feel safe." Alice laughed.

"Of course you don't, Alice. You're a freaking sharpshooter!" Maggie said.

"What?" I asked, surprised as I stared at the elegant and slim woman with the black hair piled on her head in a messy bun.

"I'm not a sharpshooter; I'm a competitive shooter."

"She's won like every competition she's even been in. You should see all her trophies."

"Get out!" Holly leaned forward. "I didn't know that!"

"It's true." Maggie nodded quickly. "She showed me a video of one of her competitions. I was amazed."

"How long have you been doing that?" I asked Alice.

"Since I was eight."

"Holy crap!" I replied.

"What does Jake think about your shooting? With as much experience as you have, you could teach firearms classes."

"Why would I tell Jake?"

"Wait." Holly's mouth fell open. "He doesn't know?"

"Are you serious? How can he not know?" Maggie continued questioning Alice after she shook her head.

"Because I have never told him. Why would I? I told you that I didn't like the man. I work for him because I like the company and the other guys. I could do without Jake and his attitude."

"You're telling me that if Jake tried to get you in bed, you wouldn't jump in headfirst?" Maggie gave her a skeptical look. "I'm not sure I could say no to that man, and I have Greg keeping my bed warm."

Alice grinned at her. "I almost went out with Greg once."

"You did?" I wondered if Maggie would be upset, but she didn't seem to be. "Did he ask you out?"

"Oh, we flirted a lot, but that stopped the moment you two reconnected at the coffee shop."

Maggie snickered. "I realize that you veered off the original question about sleeping with Jake."

Alice blinked a couple of times and then sat back. "I'm not sure Jake could handle me."

"What do you mean? How could that man not handle you?" Holly asked her and then laughed as she glanced toward me, chuckling. "I might even let him manhandle me."

Alice gnawed on her bottom lip for a moment. "You all don't know this about me, but I might be a little strong for him."

"What does that mean?" I asked, immediately picturing a scrawny, short guy.

Alice pursed her lips, and Maggie slapped her hand down on the table. "No way! You're a Dom!"

Alice turned to her, a brow raised, and Holly's jaw dropped again. "Is she right? Are you a dominatrix?"

I know my eyes almost popped out of my head. That would be the last thing I would ever consider with Alice. She looked so sweet and sexy, although she also looked exotic and fierce, too.

Alice shrugged. "I've been known to dabble."

"Holy crap!" Holly clapped her hand over her mouth. "How does that work?"

Maggie turned to Holly. "Could you imagine Jake being submissive?"

"Never!"

Alice pointed at Holly. "And that right there is why I would never sleep with Jake. He would never comply with my wishes, and I would refuse him when he would try to control me."

"I'd pay good money to see that," Maggie said.

For the rest of dinner, I listened to them talk about some of the guys they worked with, and Maggie filled me in on how she had come back in contact with her high school sweetheart.

By the time I got home that night, I was exhausted and slightly drunk. I crawled in bed and, for the first time in a few hours, started to think about the dances that I'd had earlier tonight.

I thought back over all three of them or as much of them as I could remember. Between my intoxication and the nerves I'd had earlier, it was hard to remember too many details. Somewhere in between dance two and three, I drifted off to sleep.

* * *

THE NEXT MORNING, I made myself a gourmet breakfast and then headed down to the studio, luckily without a hangover. After makeup and another big cup of coffee, Tarin joined me to record my part before the men arrived.

I chose the two that I wanted to dance with again, then stood in a back room as the three men came up the stairs and lifted their boxes. I could see them and their reactions, but I couldn't hear them. They had no idea that I was watching either.

So when the first dancer arrived, and I saw him again, I had the chance to study him for a moment. He was an attractive man, and today he wore cargo pants and a tight t-shirt that made his chest and shoulders look broader. He moved directly to the box, but before he lifted it, he closed his eyes for a moment, and I swear he seemed nervous as he pulled the invite out of the envelope.

His eyes lit up, and he grinned, and I found myself biting my bottom lip as I stared at his smile. He most definitely had a very sexy smile. He lifted the card, said something to the camera, and then glanced around briefly before he grinned and headed to the stairs.

Okay, good reaction! Had he looked around because he knew I had been watching?

The second man came up a while later, and he was wearing jeans and a polo. He was cute, but I realized that I was more attracted to the first guy. The man lifted the box and frowned. He dropped the box on the table, shrugged, and said something to the camera before he hit the stairs.

His reaction made me realize that I had been right about him. As I waited for the third man to come up, I wrung my hands. He was a really tall man, and his shoulders were broad. He just screamed safety to me, and I frowned. Why did I need a man to make me feel safe? I didn't, but it would be nice to be held in big strong arms.

Although dancer number one had a firm grip when he had held me. I'd feel safe in his arms too, and cherished, and a little sexy—maybe a whole lot of sexy.

I watched dancer number three check his box, and his smile burst out when he saw the invite. He looked pleased as he took the stairs down, and a few minutes later, Holly came up.

"What did you think of their reactions?"

"I think I chose correctly."

"I do too. Are you leaning more toward one or three?"

I laughed and put my hands over my face. "I have no idea!"

"Alright, well, you get out of here, and we will start your new routine on Monday morning."

"What is the next routine like?"

Holly grinned. "I can't tell you, but I have seen it, and you are going to love it!"

"Alright, I'm going to trust you." The two of us headed toward the stairs as the production crew went about gathering all the gear. A bunch of dancers appeared out of nowhere and headed into classrooms on the second floor.

"Any word about the restaurant?"

"No. I hope to hear something soon. I was told that I should hear by one. If so, I can be open tonight on a reduced menu at five." As we reached the first floor, my cellphone began to ring, and I pulled it out of my purse. "This is it!"

I answered the phone quickly and found Mr. Rushmore on the other end. "The tests came back negative."

"I knew they would. So I can open tonight."

"Yes. You can open, but if we get another report, you will be closed down longer."

"You aren't going to receive another complaint, at least not from my kitchen."

"Yeah, we'll see." He grunted and hung up.

"We are open. I gotta run. I'll see you Monday morning, Holly."

"Good luck," she told me as I hustled out the door, sending a text to my kitchen crew group message on my phone.

Kitchen open. Report to work ASAP to prepare.

Within a few moments, I started receiving thumbs-ups and okays, and I hailed the first cab I saw and felt better than I had in a long time as I sat in the back. For a moment, I dwelled over the two men I had chosen to have second dates with, but as the cab grew closer to the restaurant, my mindset changed, and I began to plan the menu and how things would have to go tonight to make sure we didn't have any further problems.

CHAPTER THIRTEEN

HARVEY

"Y ou really got picked?" Greg asked when I called him later that day.

"Yeah, I did."

"Okay, that's pretty cool, I guess. Maggie said she was a nice lady."

"What else did she say?"

I heard Maggie yelling in the background for him to keep his mouth shut. "Sorry, man, I've been sworn to secrecy."

"It's a good thing that I don't have a problem with suspense," I joked back.

"Yeah, that is good. So what do you need me to take over this week for you?"

"I'm supposed to be at the dance studio from eleven to two each day."

"Do you want me to cover the entire class for you? That way, you don't have to sweat it if you are running late or get a run in your stockings?"

"Ha ha! Yeah, that might work better. What do you have going on at the office? I can cover what you got going on there."

We talked for a few minutes about trading caseloads, and

then I spent the rest of the day cleaning my house, doing laundry, and working out. All afternoon, I found myself smiling and hoping that the next dance went as well as the first one did.

* * *

MONDAY MORNING, I was back at the dance studio and went directly to the room where they did the makeup. I was almost done when my sister popped her head inside.

"Hey, sorry we didn't get a chance to have dinner this weekend. It got a little hectic with trying to get all the footage edited."

"That's okay. I hope you made me look good in the edits."

She grinned. "Harv, you don't need any help looking good."

The lady doing my hair chuckled. "No, he does not. I barely have anything to do with this one."

"I'll see you in the other room in a few minutes."

After I was finished with makeup and wardrobe, which consisted of getting fitted with my microphone, we started recording immediately. I joined Tarin, Cal, and Clara in the main room where hugs went all around as they welcomed me back.

"Are you as nervous this time as you were last time?" Tarin asked.

"Not yet, but I'm sure I'll get there as we get closer. I'm just glad that I wasn't the only one to feel something when we were dancing."

"The sparks between you too were off the charts," Cal said. "Are you ready to hear the song for your next dance?"

"Yep! I can't wait."

"Alright," Tarin said and nodded to someone off the set. The music started, and I knew the song immediately.

"This is by Ed Sheeran; this is a great song." I rubbed my hands together as I shifted back and forth on my feet. "Big change from a fast fun song to a slow romantic one."

"As much fun as the first dance was, we want to slow things down for you guys. This one is all about trusting one another. Do you want to see the routine?"

I was totally up for a slow song, and I was raring to be able to hold her closer. "Bring it on."

Clara took her place, and Victor came out to assist her. I'd learned that Victor was my date's current training partner. As they started, I found myself excited, but very quickly, that feeling changed to anxiety. "Holy crap," I said about a dozen times when they did stunts, or he lifted Clara, spinning her this way and that. How the hell was I going to be able to do that in only a few days?

When they finished, I stood there catching flies with my mouth wide open, and Cal chuckled. "You look a little over-whelmed, Harvey."

"A little? You expect me to do that?" I asked him as I rubbed the side of my face. "Is there any part of her body that I won't be touching?"

Everyone laughed. "Not many," Cal answered, and Victor agreed with a chuckle.

Tarin put her arm around my shoulders. "What makes you the most nervous about this routine?"

I laughed. "Everything. I'm not sure I can do all that. That's a really long routine."

"You can do it, Harv," Tarin said, and Cal nodded.

"You can. I promise that you will master this and do it excep-tionally well. If you notice Victor, he's not making a lot of diffi-cult moves. His job is to support Clara and allow her to do most of the work. Don't get me wrong, your part in this is crucial, and the dance won't look or feel nearly as beautiful and sexy if you aren't strong enough to handle it, but I have faith in you."

I shook my head. "Normally, I'm a pretty confident guy, but not right now. I'm glad that you all have confidence in me."

"Well, let's get started, and I think your confidence will

grow," Cal stated and began to explain the beginning of the routine and how we will walk toward one another.

The routine was almost five minutes long, so I was going to have to learn a minute and forty seconds of it each day. On Thursday, I would run through the dance in its entirety over and over again until I had it down pat, and then on Friday, I would rehearse it with Clara at another site before the taped dance. At least this time, we didn't have any outside influence like we did at the park. The dances would be filmed inside at a hotel using their ballroom.

I ended up staying an hour later on Monday to keep practicing in a small room with Clara. My competition wasn't coming in until five, so I was glad to have some extra time. On Tuesday, I practiced with Clara another two hours after we finished taping.

I had asked her how the other guy was doing since she was also working with him in the evenings, and she said that he was picking it up quickly. Being the competitive person that I was, that answer frustrated me, but she told me that I had come a long way since we started.

By the end of Wednesday, I thought that I had an excellent grasp on the dance, and I looked forward to going through the entire thing the next day. How strange it was that this dance—scratch that—this whole thing had consumed me. When I was at work, I had a hard time concentrating on anything, and I'd made Alice and Maggie dance with me on a few of the moves to make sure I had the footing right and wasn't confusing the steps with something else.

I was at the office early Thursday morning, sipping from my green smoothie when Jake stuck his head around the corner of my cubby. "You got a minute, twinkle toes?"

I shook my head at him. "Yes, I can give you a minute. I can even give you a couple of minutes if you stand in for my training partner and help me with part of my routine."

"Not on your life, sweet cheeks! Meet me in my office in five, and put the coffee on."

"Coffee is already on," I told him as he walked away. "You can pour your cup as you walk by it."

"Fine."

A few minutes later, I was taking a seat in his office. "You have something against dancing?"

"What? No, not really. It's not very masculine, but hey, whatever."

I laughed. "Jake, man, you should see the stuff that I have to do in this dance. I'm lifting the girl and spinning her around. I'll be lucky if I don't drop her or get puked on when I make her dizzy. It's more of a workout than some of my trips to the gym."

"That intense?"

"Yeah. You should come on Friday and watch it."

He grinned. "You're going to let me have a front-row seat to watch you go up in flames?"

"Ha! I don't know why I invited you, other than I am working my ass off and could use some support. I'm nervous as hell on this one. The first one was relatively easy and fun. This one is a whole lot more work, and damn, it's sexy as hell."

"What do you mean sexy?"

"This girl is going to be in my arms, and there is probably nowhere on her body that I won't be touching. I'm serious; it's a really sexy song."

"Hmm, maybe I'll have to come." He paused. "Alice going to be there?"

"Why? You want to try the dance out on her?" I smirked his way.

"No, I'm not interested in Alice. Why does everyone think that?"

"If you aren't interested in her, then why did you ask if she would be there?"

He shrugged. "Alice is not my type."

"Your type?" I barked out a laugh. "Dude, you two would be explosive together. It's so funny that you both deny it, but all of us see it."

"You guys are making shit up. Can we focus on work now? I wanted to talk to you about a trip we will be making next month. Or are you going to be changing careers and dancing full time now?"

"You're a shithead. Talk."

Jake and I discussed business for about an hour, and we decided that I would head it up since it was another humanitarian mission to deliver more medical supplies. Greg and Maggie would be going with me—the first one that she would officially be going on—and Brett, Wyatt, and Drake would also be coming along.

I glanced at my watch. "I gotta get going. Today is the dress rehearsal."

He shook his head as he laughed. "What time is this competition tomorrow?"

"Not sure, but I'll let you know."

"Go break a leg or something." He waved me out of his office as his desk phone rang.

I turned my computer off and grabbed my keys from my desk before I stopped by Maggie's office. "I hear you are going with us on our next trip."

Her eyes sparkled. "Are you serious? Did he just tell you that?"

"He did."

Maggie jumped out of her chair and threw her arms around me. "Thank you!"

"Don't thank me, thank Jake."

"Are you dancing with my woman again?" Greg asked from the door as I stepped back from Maggie.

"I get to go!" she said excitedly.

"Go where?" He looked confused.

"On the mission next month."

"Ah, good stuff." He grinned at her as she rushed past him and down the hallway.

"How come you got a hug, and I got brushed past?" Greg asked as she disappeared down the hallway.

I snickered. "Because I gave her the good news. What are you doing here? Why aren't you teaching the class today?"

"I had to come by and pick something up. Our handouts were missing. Alice made new ones for me."

"Ah, how is the class going?"

"Probably better than your dancing." He slapped me on the back as we headed toward the front door.

"Hey, now! I'll have you know that I'm a good dancer."

He chuckled. "How is it going?"

"Well, I'm about to head out and do the dress rehearsal. So far, I have been doing pieces of it; now I'm going to do the entire thing a few times."

"You think you have it down?"

"Yeah, but I also think one wrong move and I could screw the entire thing up."

"You'll do fine."

"I hope so. You coming to watch tomorrow?"

"I don't think Maggie would let me miss it." He grinned.

"Alright, I'll see you tomorrow then."

"You got it." I waved to Alice, and I was on my way. When I arrived at the hotel where we would be doing the filming the next night, I found myself almost as nervous as I had been last Friday. This was only a dress rehearsal, and I was a nervous wreck. What was I going to be like tomorrow?

I changed into slacks, dress shoes, and a button-down shirt, then joined the crew in the ballroom. I stood there, staring at the dance floor, and my stomach did a flip. What made me think that I could do this, or that doing this would somehow show a woman that I was right for her?

For the first time in almost two weeks, I began to question why I was doing this. Clara joined me, pulling my arm. "You are looking freaked out. Let's just get out there and let the music flow. You know this, Harv, and you are going to do amazing."

"If you say so."

We took our places, and I could feel my knees shaking. I'd never been so nervous in my life. The music started, and we began. We had to stop and redo things the first couple of times, but by the fourth one, I was on a roll. It was smooth, and I was having fun. I could do this, and I just hoped that tomorrow when I did it with my new dance partner, I did it just as well.

"I think you got it," Clara held her hands up, and I gave her a high five.

"I could not have done this if I didn't have such a great partner. Speaking of partners, how is she doing with this routine?"

Clara glanced around. "We aren't supposed to talk about it, but I heard she really nailed it. Which is surprising because she's not a dancer, but I guess she had some in her blood after all."

"Well, that's good."

"I think you two are going to really do well together," she whispered toward me. "My money is on you, by the way. I can see you two together and cannot wait to see you two dance this routine tomorrow. It's going to be spectacular."

"Thanks for that, Clara. That means a lot."

She hugged me. "Don't let me down now!"

"I won't." My sister joined us, and Clara quickly said her goodbyes.

"Well, how do you feel about all of this?"

"I was nervous as hell when I got here today, but now that I have done the whole thing a few times, I feel a lot more confident."

"You looked good out there, Harvey. Surprised the hell out of me that you could dance."

I chuckled. "Yeah, I kind of surprised myself too."

"What are you going to do if she picks you after this?"

"What do you mean, what am I going to do?"

"I mean, are you going to go out with her?"

"Sure. That's what this is all about, right? You can only tell so much from dancing with one another. If she picks me, then I'd like to see what might be there."

My sister looked like she was about to explode with excitement. "Okay. Then you better go home and get your beauty sleep. You don't want to scare her away tomorrow."

CHAPTER FOURTEEN

ALI

*W*ork was nuts. Luckily Saturday night had been slower than usual because people hadn't been sure we'd be open. People that did come in were either diehard customers or didn't have any clue that we'd been under suspicion in the first place. A few customers asked how things were going, and what caused the shutdown, but Anton was able to brush all of that away.

In the kitchen, we took extra precautions. We had sanitized everything with a deep cleaning and then gotten to work preparing for the night. Our menu was adjusted to fit what we could quickly cook without hours of extra preparation, and what we had in stock, along with a few recipes that we were introducing on a special menu that we called a testing menu. We tried to make the customers feel special by saying they were part of our surprise test group, and I was out of the kitchen on and off during the night to check on their opinions. I was also watching my staff like a hawk.

Not that I thought any of them had done something wrong, but I couldn't take the chance that it would happen again. By the time the night was over, I was exhausted. At midnight, I was walking in my door, and I was asleep on my feet.

Sunday was more of the same, and it was another stressful night, but at least we were back to our regular menu, for the most part. There were a few things that we weren't able to get in fresh, but we were back in business. I spoke to Randolph as soon as I woke and let him know how things were going. He didn't seem concerned and told me that he knew I could handle it. That is why he had hired me as the head chef. That made me feel a little better, but it still irked me that we had been blamed for food poisoning when there had been no proof found.

On Sundays, we opened at four instead of five, but we also closed an hour earlier. I was home and in bed by eleven, and while I was excited about this next week of dancing, I was also dreading it. I had never imagined that it would be so physically grueling.

* * *

DID I seriously think just last night that the past week had been physically grueling? Holy crap! I stood in the dance studio, my jaw hanging open as I watched Clara and Victor move around the room. They expected me to do that? There was no way I could do half of what they were asking, and I sure as hell could not look even half as sexy as she did.

I knew that Clara was the dance partner to the two men, and I wondered what she thought of them. What would they think of me after dancing with her? She was grace and style, and her body was so fluid and oozed sex. I couldn't do that.

I spun around and started walking toward the door. I heard Holly yell, "Cut!" and then a hand grabbed my arm and pulled me around.

"Where do you think you are going?" Cal asked although he looked very concerned.

"I can't do that, Cal! There is no way I could do that dance. She makes it look so easy, but I can't do that! The way she flips her hair and brushes her body against him. You expect me to do that with two men that I don't even know? I cannot do that! Or —or trust them to flip me over their back, hold me as they spin in a circle, and lift me like that? There is no way!"

Holly appeared at my side. "Ali, you can do this! This dance was made for you."

"Made me for me? Are you nuts? This dance was made for sexy and sophisticated. I am neither."

"Cal, can you give us a moment?" He nodded and stepped aside as Holly led me over to the corner.

"I know you don't think you can do this, Ali, but I know you can. I can picture you doing it. Now you need to picture it. Isn't this exactly what you wanted—a dance to get you out of your comfort zone and show people that you are a sexy woman with more than your food?"

I pursed my lips and hugged myself. "Holly, how the hell can I trust these men to hold me like that? Jesus, they are touching almost every part of my body. I don't even know these men."

"I agree that it is a very touchy dance, but you can't tell me that it didn't intrigue you just a little bit. Put aside your fear for a moment, and picture those two men that you danced with last week. Don't you think they are going to be afraid of not being good enough for you? Can you picture either of those men giving up?"

I considered that for a moment. Both of those men had been determined and reliable and also fun. Would they be able to pull this off and add in the sexual and romantic elements? Would we all look like bumbling idiots? At least if we were I wouldn't be alone in this.

Holly took my shoulders. "I will promise you that both of these guys are going to be just as afraid as you are. But I know they are going to do it because they are both determined to make you happy and see if that connection grows. It's going to be tough, but I know you can do this, Ali."

"There is no way I can look anywhere as sexy as she does." I nodded toward Clara, who was chatting with Victor and Cal.

"You will. I promise you. Once you get the hang of it and get comfortable with this dance, you will add your own sexuality to it."

I laughed abruptly, and everyone glanced my way. "I can't believe I am going to do this."

"You got this, Ali."

"If you say so," I muttered, and then she pulled me back to Cal and Tarin, who gave me more of a pep talk.

"Alright, let's go back to the end of the dance and get a new reaction from Ali," Holly called.

I closed my eyes, inhaled deeply, and shook out my arms, nodding toward Holly that I was ready. The music ended, and Tarin turned to me. "What do you think?"

My knees were shaking, but I forced a smile. "I think I have a lot of work to do."

They left it at that, and we quickly started to learn the dance. Clara stayed around to help me, and we worked on ten to fifteen seconds of the dance at a time. I struggled with a few steps, but I forced myself to stay focused and work hard. By ten that morning, I had learned almost the first two minutes of the dance. I still had problems with some of the moves, but I knew what I was supposed to do.

* * *

MY CELLPHONE RANG a few hours later, and I glanced at the name to see it was Charlie. "Hey, are you back in town?" I asked as I walked into the small office in the back of the kitchen.

"Yes, I am—what a whirlwind. I'm so sorry that I wasn't there for you Friday. How did the dance go?"

"That's okay. It went well, and now I'm learning another dance for this week."

"Any idea which one of the guys you will choose?"

"No, not yet."

"What are they like?"

I chuckled. "I don't know. They are both handsome. One has bright green eyes, and the other has blue eyes. One has dark hair, the other blond. Both are strong, although the second one is a bit more built. They both have fantastic smiles."

"Did either of them make your heart beat faster?"

I laughed harder. "Charlie, we were dancing; my heart was hammering in my chest! The routine was super energetic, but holy crap, nothing like this week's dance."

"What song are you dancing to this week?"

"Ed Sheeran's 'Thinking Out Loud.'"

"Oh, I love that song. That is a very romantic song."

"Wait till you see the dance."

"Is it romantic?"

"It is, but it's also very sexy, and the dancing is crazy. I've only learned a portion of it, and I'm kind of amazed that I can do some of what they are asking me to do."

"Come on, Ali, you know you can do anything you put your mind to."

"In the kitchen!"

"Just think of it as a different kind of cooking."

"Very funny."

"Will I be able to watch this week?"

"Yes, I put you on the list."

"Great, I can't wait to see you and check out the two guys."

We talked a little more about it, and then they needed me in the kitchen. As usual, the night flew by, and before I knew it, it was Thursday morning.

My body ached in every possible joint it could. I stood under the hot shower spray after I woke up, trying to get my muscles to relax enough to stretch. I only had to get through two more days of this, and it would be over.

What would I have then? Would I find a man that I could build a life with? Or was this all just a colossal waste of time? What if I choose wrong? What if the one I thought would be good for me wasn't the right one? I'll never know. I signed a contract that said I would only date the man I chose for at least one month. Not that I had to stay with him that entire month, but I wasn't allowed to be seen with any other men, especially either of the other dancers, until after the show aired.

If I picked wrong, would the other man even be interested in getting to know me? Did I even want to date anyone?

I sighed as I turned off the water. I needed to get through this and see what happened. If I picked wrong, then I chose wrong, and life would go on. Maybe someday I would find the right man.

I dried my hair and told myself that I needed to focus on getting the dance down without breaking anything, and then I could worry about my future love life.

At the hotel, I found Victor, who hugged me tightly. "I think you are going to be pleasantly surprised by your dance partners."

"Why do you say that?" I asked as I pulled back.

"Clara told me that they have done fantastic in the last two days. Better than she ever expected."

I sighed. "So, I'm the only one that is going to look stupid then, is that what you are saying?"

He laughed and took hold of my face. "You will look anything but stupid, Ali. You have taken to this routine as if it were designed specifically for you."

I stared at him sideways. "Why are you trying to butter me up?"

He laughed. "I'm not buttering you up. After you do a few

run-throughs today, you'll get to see it on screen, and you will see that you are better than you thought."

"Yeah, we'll see about that."

While I had done almost the whole dance at one time, today was the first time I had gone from start to finish without pausing. It was exhausting, but also a little exhilarating as people worked on the lighting around us. Victor and I did it three times before Holly pulled me over to a bank of computer monitors and let me watch it.

I was amazed at what I saw. "Holy cow, I actually do look good."

Victor threw his arm around me. "I told you. You're better than you think you are."

I had Holly pause it a few times, and we talked over a couple of moves. I could see where I was slightly stilted and where I needed to add a bit more of a flourish to flirt more openly. After we watched it three times, I went back out, and Victor and I danced two more times.

"How do you feel about it?" Tarin asked on camera.

"About as good as I can. I know the steps, and now I just have to trust the men that I will be dancing with will know them too and not drop me."

"I don't think you'll have a problem with that." They cut and I was rushed out to make room for my male partner number one. How much I wished I could have peeked into the room to watch him, but I was forced to leave.

As I took a taxi to the restaurant, I found myself smiling. I couldn't believe that I looked as good as I did. I was no Clara, that's for sure, but I appeared to know what I was doing, and I looked smooth and sexy while doing it. Now I only had to do it two more times—and make a decision that could be life-altering. No pressure there.

CHAPTER FIFTEEN

HARVEY

I couldn't sit still, so I paced the room. I was in a suite upstairs at the hotel, and I wandered back and forth between the bedroom, bathroom, and the sitting room. Two production staff were seated in the living room area, probably to keep me from jetting out of here.

How many contestants had tried to do that at the last minute —or would I be the first? A knock sounded on the door, and I wandered back into the bedroom area, assuming it was more production staff when I heard my name called and stuck my head around the doorjamb.

Greg was grinning over Maggie's head as they entered, and behind them were Alex and Lexi, Trevor and Davina, Mike, Alice, Wyatt, Joe, and Jake.

"Damn, the gang's all here." I joined the group and collected hugs and back slaps. When I turned, Lexi was studying me carefully.

I raised a brow toward her as I waited for whatever comment was about to come out of her mouth. "They did a nice job on your eyes."

I chuckled. "You think she will like me without all this makeup on?"

"Oh, please!" Maggie said. "She is going to like you any way you come."

There were a few twitters around the group, and Alice and Lexi rolled their eyes. "You guys are such little boys sometimes," Maggie said, then turned to me. "Are you ready to go out there and knock her dead?"

"Jesus, Maggie, don't say that. I might drop her on her head and kill her."

She smacked my arm. "That's not what I meant, and you know it."

"It could happen."

"You nervous?" Trevor asked.

"Yep." I nodded dramatically. "I think I am more nervous about this five-minute dance than I ever was for any combat mission I undertook."

"Yeah." Jake laughed. "That's because love is worse than war."

I peered at Alice—well, most of us glanced her way—but she just stared back at me with no expression on her face. She was kind of amazing like that—I think you called that being unflappable.

"What would you even know about love?" Trevor asked Jake. "It's not like you have ever been in love before."

"Yes, I have!"

"Yeah, loving yourself and using your hand is not being in love," Wyatt said, and everyone cut up laughing.

"Mr. Melton," someone said from behind me. "It's time to head down."

"Aww." Trevor grinned at me. "Our little boy is going off to find love on the dance floor."

"Get out of here," I snapped back at him playfully.

Everyone wished me well and threw me some taunts about breaking a leg and not paralyzing the poor girl before they said their goodbyes. I asked the production guys to give me a minute and went into the bedroom.

I sat down on the edge of the bed, closed my eyes, and tried to slow my breathing that had begun to gain momentum the minute they said it was time. Please do not let me drop this woman, and if it's meant to be, let it be.

I slapped my thighs as I stood and stared at my reflection. "I got this."

Downstairs, a lot was going on. More cameras, more crew, and this time, there was a small audience in a side room, where large television screens were up so bystanders could watch the filming. I heard Alex laughing as I walked by. I peered in and saw about thirty people milling around.

Holly found me as I entered another room. "Are you ready?"

"Yes."

She hugged me tightly. "I know you will do great, Harv."

"Thanks."

"Are you nervous?"

"Very."

She laughed. "I don't think I have ever seen you nervous before. Who knew a date would get you this worked up."

"It's more than a date, Holly. It's dancing in front of all these people, and not dropping her while trying to make a connection."

Holly glanced around and stepped closer, lowering her voice. "Harv, you be yourself out there, and this will be perfect." She kissed my cheek. "I'm pulling for you."

She gave me a nudge toward the side and told me to prepare myself. It wasn't five minutes later that they were getting me settled just inside the darkened room. In the center of the dance floor, there was one spotlight lit. You could see nothing on the other side, and I tried my hardest, knowing that she was over there. Was she as nervous as I was?

When the music started, we would walk toward one another

and meet in the center of the light before a few other lights came up. My heart threatened to explode from my chest, and I wiped my hands down my pants.

Oh, shit—shit—shit!

What the hell was I doing? What if I forgot the dance? What if I dropped her? What if I did all this, and it was for nothing? I put my hand to the collar of my shirt, and even though it wasn't buttoned at the top, I tugged on it as if I couldn't breathe. I forced myself to swallow.

For a second, I froze. What if she didn't pick me? I wanted her to pick me. I wanted her to choose me. I didn't like to lose.

A soft male voice sounded off to my side. "Ready, and three, two, one." A palm in the center of my back gently pushed me forward just as the music began to play. Five steps later, I reached the dance floor. I could just make her out on the opposite side. We stepped in unison again, and my fears vanished as I began to make out her features. I dropped my chin to my chest, staring at the ground as I took the last few steps as was my part in all this.

A light-purple gauzy dress flowed around her pretty legs, and her feet were bare. Her toes were dainty and painted the same color as her dress. *Please don't let me step on her toes.* Her small hand landed on my chest, her fingernails also light purple, and I couldn't help but smile as I began to lift my face but snapped it to the side as she took my hand and placed her right hand into it. I curled my fingers around her warm skin, and she lifted my chin with the tips of her fingers, her touch sending waves of something warm through my chest. Our eyes made contact for the first time, and I felt electrified.

For a few beats, we stared at one another. I wanted to pick her up right then and run away with her, but a moment later, she broke eye contact as she spun to the side away from me and began to move through the routine. There were no other thoughts besides taking every step with her, being beside her.

When I wasn't thinking about what came next, I was thinking about how beautiful she was with her dark wavy hair coursing down her back and that sexy dress wrapped around her body. The moves came without effort—almost without thought—as I lifted her with ease and treasured every moment that our bodies were in contact. I spun her around, I lifted her, I held her, and just before she'd move away again, I'd feel a pain in my chest as if I knew what was coming and didn't want it to.

At one point, we turned toward one another, meaning to come nose to nose, but we were so close that our lips brushed, and I heard her gasp slightly as she twirled away from me. My lips tingled from the slight touch and continued to do so for another few seconds.

She was elegant and beautiful, and she entranced me down to my soul. During one point in the song, we were both on the ground, and I pulled her to me. I could instantly imagine having her there in the crook of my arm for years to come, but in another beat of the song, she was up and moving playfully away.

I loved touching her, loved the feel of her body as it slipped down or slithered around me. I adored the smiles on her face as she peered at me through her lashes, almost shyly, but also seductively as if begging me to be the man she needed—the man she had dreamed of having.

There was one move that I feared slightly, and it was one of the hardest steps for her. She would lie on the floor, and her legs would wrap around my waist as I began to lift her. Only she would be doing most of the work as she slowly curled herself from a backbend up and around me.

She made it seem effortless, and she fit so perfectly against me that I never wanted to let her go.

When we came to the final step, her knee was against my hip, and one hand was curled under her thigh to hold it in place. Her arms were wrapped around my neck, and our faces were only an inch apart. Both of us were breathing hard, but smiling as we stared at one another.

I didn't want to let her go, didn't want to watch her walk away, and I cupped her cheek, pulling her lips to mine. I hadn't meant to kiss her. I'd never even considered it, but as I started to do it, I knew I needed to. This might be the only time I would get the chance, and I needed her to know what I was feeling just then.

She kissed me back for a few brief seconds, and then it was over. We snapped out of it and began to pull back, each of us startled that we had just done that. We stared at one another. Was she as shocked as I was to be sucked so deeply into the moment? Had she too forgotten where we were? Had she wanted to kiss me too?

I let her leg go, and it slowly brushed down mine as she began to step away. One hand caressed my cheek for only a second before it dropped to her side, and she turned and rushed off the floor. I felt so suddenly lost that I didn't know what to do, and then remembered that I needed to go back the way I had come. Only, my body wanted to follow hers.

The crew was there to direct me out the door to the hallway. As I stepped out, I turned back to the door, but it was closing. I shifted around to the camera in a daze.

"That was—that was amazing. I've never felt anything like that before." I wiped my hands down my face, still trying to catch my breath. "She was incredible—beautiful and graceful, and so damn sexy. I'm not sure there will ever be another moment in life like this one."

I had to wait a few moments, and when Tarin joined me, I still hadn't collected myself. "How do you feel after that?"

"I don't know how to feel, Tarin. It's like I just danced with an angel, and she stole a piece of my soul."

"An angel?"

"Yes. She didn't just dance, she floated. She was so elegant, so beautiful; she took my breath away."

"I have to ask you, Harvey. Did you plan on kissing her when the dance started?"

I shook my head. "No, not at all. Earlier on in the routine, our lips brushed, and mine tingled for a while, but that was an accident. I've never had anyone do that to me before. In the end, when we finished, it wasn't a conscious choice; it was just something that I needed to do. It was like the final move to the most perfect moment of my life."

"It was perfect—even the kiss was perfect, Harvey. It was straight out of a movie. I think every woman here swooned slightly."

I chuckled.

"Alright, we need to move you along, so she can get ready to do her second dance. How do you feel about that?"

"I can't imagine them having the kind of connection that we did."

"I guess we will see."

As I stepped away, Holly rushed me and threw her arms around my neck. "That was amazing, Harvey. You two looked so beautiful out there. So perfect together, almost professional. How do you feel?"

"To be honest, I feel a little overwhelmed." I laughed slightly. "I'm not sure how to feel."

"Well, if she doesn't pick you, she's crazy!" she said softly. "Now, you need to go because they are bringing the other guy down."

"Can I watch?"

"No!" she said quickly. "You need to go back upstairs, and then you can meet up with everyone after. They can tell you how the second dance went, and you will get to see some clips of the dance from the center point."

"You are no fun." I kissed her cheek and headed back to the

elevator. I was just getting on when the elevator across from us opened, and a man with another camera crew stepped out. Our eyes locked, and there was no doubt he knew who I was. He nodded once, and then my door closed.

He was tall and muscular. He was also very blond with his hair longer than mine and parted on the side, and I noticed immediately how blue his eyes were. He was kind of like a Nordic God, so opposite of my athletic body, dark hair, and trim beard.

I hope he drops her, I thought to myself and then winced. I didn't want the woman to get hurt. As we got inside the hotel room, I went right to the bar and poured myself a whiskey, tossing it back and then refilling the glass as a couple of the guys behind me chuckled. I didn't regularly drink hard liquor, but tonight I was making an exception.

The next hour was probably the longest hour of my life. By the time my gang came up to me, I was well on my way to being drunk.

"Harvey, if I knew you could dance that well, I would have never gotten involved with Alex," Lexi said as she kissed my cheek. "You were so smooth, so perfect!"

Everyone had something to say about my dance, but no one said anything about the second dance. Waiters showed up with food, and everyone began to mill about and enjoy it before I finally lost my patience and yelled to get everyone's attention.

"Come on! Someone tell me how the other dance went? Was their dance better?"

Jake laughed. "Well, I don't know. He didn't try to have sex with her in the middle of the floor."

"I didn't try to have sex with her," I stated, confused. "Are you saying that they didn't dance as well together?"

Alice sighed and stepped forward. "No one here is going to tell you the truth, but they did look good together. They danced just as well as you two did."

"Did it look like she liked him more?"

Trevor cracked up. "Dude, they were dancing. Who knows which one of you she might like better."

"I don't get how you are supposed to like someone by just dancing with them," Joe said.

Wyatt shrugged. "Me either."

I ignored the guys and turned back to Alice. "Did he kiss her?"

"No," Maggie said as she stepped forward and put her hand on my arm. "He didn't, and they didn't stand there looking at one another as long as you two did. I think you have a good chance of being picked."

"You think so?"

"Yeah, you got a fifty-fifty chance," Trevor joked and stepped around me to get more food.

"You are no help."

"When do you find out?" Maggie asked.

"Sunday," I replied.

"Well, Trevor is right," Alice said. "You have a fifty percent chance that she will pick you. Unless you scared her away with the kiss."

Would that count against me? It wasn't like it had been planned. It had come out of nowhere because it had been a natural reaction. We were dancing, and it just seemed like the perfect time to share that first kiss with her. What if I screwed up my chances by following my heart on that one?

Shit! I stepped to the side and sank into a chair. I probably did. I most likely ruined my chances by doing that. She probably thinks I'm some sex-starved maniac who kisses strangers all the time.

"Hey, stop beating yourself up. Personally, if that had been me, I would pick the hot guy who laid a scorching hot kiss on me over the guy who just grinned," Alice said. "Let's just hope you swept her off her feet."

CHAPTER SIXTEEN

ALI

I touched my lips as I rounded the corner and stared at the camera. "Did that just happen?"

There was some laughter around me, and I turned and looked back at the closed door. "Did that really just happen? Did I just kiss him?"

Tarin stepped up to me. "Well, you tell me. What do you think just happened?"

"I think I just danced the most exciting dance of my life, and then this gorgeous and sexy man kissed me."

"Were you expecting that?"

I shook my head, my hair whipping back and forth over my shoulders. "No, not at all."

"What did you think of the dance?"

"It was incredible." I was somewhat awestruck that I had just danced that with a stranger. For some reason, I had expected Victor to be there stepping into the light. It had startled me, but the moment I touched him, I came to life. My entire body had felt energized, and the dance became almost effortless—fun—not work.

Our lips had brushed earlier in the routine, an accidental

touch that had left my head spinning slightly, but nothing like how it felt now. How could I dance with a stranger and have such feelings inside of me?

"Well, you need to get back to your dressing area and take a break. Get freshened up and clear your mind because you need to do that again."

"Holy cow! I can't believe I have to do that again." I shook my hands out in front of me. How could anything compare to what I had just done? How could I look at another man the same way? I think that the first man had stolen my heart from my chest. He sure made it beat hard enough to break free.

But I did dance. I danced it just as well, if not a little better the second time. It was fun and sexy, and I felt comfortable with his arms wrapped around me—with his hands on me. Although they didn't make my body tingle. He didn't try to kiss my mouth, but he did brush his lips over my forehead as he started to turn away after only a second once we finished.

I rushed off the floor as soon as he turned from me, able to think better than the first dance, but confused about my feelings. I felt things with both of them, one comfortable and safe, the other exciting and stimulating. Which one was I going to choose?

"Do you know who you are going to pick?" Tarin asked.

I shook my head quickly. "I have no clue. They were both fantastic, and I felt things with both of them. I don't know how I can choose between them."

"It's a good thing that you have a day to decide," Tarin said. The cameras turned off, and they called it a wrap for the night. Cal and Victor rushed to my side, congratulating me on a fantastic job. I had to admit that I amazed myself.

I heard my name being called and turned to see Charlie. "You made it!" I said to her as she reached me and threw her arm around me.

"Holy shit, Ali! You were fantastic!"

"Did you see both dances?"

"Yes, I arrived about five minutes before the first one. They wouldn't let me see you because you were about to go on."

The two of us went back to my dressing area. "What did you think?"

"I think you have a difficult decision to make."

"Which man do you think I danced better with?"

She pursed her lips and tapped them for a moment. "From an artist's point of view, I would say the second one. You seemed more comfortable with him, and he complemented you very well. You were like complete opposites—light and dark. What color were his eyes?"

"Blue, and I think I felt more comfortable with him. It was almost easier to do the routine with him." I paused. "So, you think I should choose him?"

"I didn't say that." She grinned like the cat that ate the canary. "I said you looked more comfortable with him."

"But you also said I danced better with him."

"Yes, because you looked comfortable. You looked like you could depend on him, trust him. Like you already know that he's going to be a good guy and safe to date."

"So? Isn't that the point. You say that like it's a bad thing."

She shook her head. "It's not a bad thing. It's a safe thing."

I removed the dress and pulled my t-shirt over my head. "What are you talking about?"

"The first guy you danced with, he was mysterious—almost —yeah, he was mysterious. He moved lithely, almost like he was stalking you."

I laughed. "Stalking me? What are you talking about, Charlie?"

"He was a very sexual animal, Ali. In fact, he oozed danger and sex."

I laughed as I shook my head and pulled on my leggings. "He did not ooze danger and sex, Char."

"He did, and oh, my god! That kiss! I was waving a hand in front of my face. The two of you melted the film! You should have heard everyone in the viewing room."

"We did not!" I felt my cheeks heating up. "And that was a surprise. I did not expect that."

"Of course you didn't expect that. He obviously didn't either, but it was like he couldn't resist. He had to taste you."

I threw my head back and laughed loudly. "He did not have to taste me. Are you drunk?"

"Only a little." She waved a hand in front of her face. "But that's not the point. He looked like he had to have you. You didn't see it, but after you turned and ran off-camera, he just stood there and stared after you. It was like you rocked his world. Like he didn't know which way was up."

I stared at her, one foot partially in my sneaker. "Are you serious? He watched me leave?"

"Yep, you were gone for a few seconds before he turned and left the floor."

I was going to tell her she must have remembered it wrong when someone knocked on the door, and Holly popped her head in the room. "I wanted to check on you before you left."

"Come on in. Holly Melton, this is my friend Charlie Yardley."

They said hello, then Holly asked her, "What did you think of her dancing?"

"She was amazing. I think she could be a professional if she ever quit cooking."

"Ha!" I threw my head back and put on my other shoe. "That's never happening."

Holly studied me for a moment. "How are you doing?"

"I'm okay, just so very confused."

"Not sure which one to pick?"

"I have no clue which one to choose, and Charlie is not being any help."

Holly and Charlie both chuckled. "I am being helpful; she just doesn't want to listen to my advice."

"What is your advice?"

"Actually, I hadn't given it to her yet. I was explaining to her that dancer number two was the safe choice, and the first guy was danger and sex—almost predatory."

Holly barked out a quick laugh. "Well, that's one way to describe him."

"Don't you agree?"

"I can't really say; I'm the producer of the show, so I can't give any opinion."

"But you have to admit that guy number one was much sexier than the second guy, right? The dark looks, the way he moved. Damn, if Ali doesn't want him, can you hook a girl up?"

"Easy now, Charlie. I haven't made my decision yet. Don't go stealing my choices before I do."

"I'm just saying if you don't want him." She cocked her head to the side. "I would photograph him in the jungle."

"What?" Holly asked, looking baffled.

"She's a photographer; she does an incredible job of finding just the right background for a subject." I turned to Charlie. "Where would you put the other guy?"

Charlie considered that for a moment and then laughed. "In a minivan with three kids and a dog in the back seat."

"Oh, come on, Charlie!" I threw my hands up in the air.

"What? You asked. He's that safe-looking."

I rolled my eyes. "Why did I ask you to come? You are no help."

"Whatever!" Charlie muttered.

Holly put her hand on my arm. "Well, tomorrow afternoon, we will have the footage ready for you, and you'll be able to watch both the first and second dance that you had with them. Maybe that will help you decide."

"I really get to see them?"

"Yep."

"Can I bring Charlie? She didn't get to see the first round."

"Sure."

"That's great. Maybe that will help me." I glanced at my watch. "Look, I'd love to stay and chat with both of you, but I need to get to the restaurant."

"You're working tonight? It's almost eight o'clock." Charlie asked.

"Yeah, but the kitchen is open for another couple of hours, and I need to make sure we are good for tomorrow."

"Alright, I'll give you a call tomorrow and let you know when we are ready."

"Perfect, thank you, Holly. Charlie, I'll call you tomorrow."

I was out the door as soon as I said goodbye, and rushing to the side exit so that I could catch a cab. I rounded the corner onto the main street and smashed right into someone, almost hitting them hard enough that I fell back. Just like the last time, a hand grabbed me and kept me from falling. My face snapped up, and I stared into the eyes of dancer number one. Immediately, the world around me disappeared.

"Get your hands off of her right this minute," I heard a woman say, and then a hand covered my eyes, and two other hands pulled me away.

"I was just trying to keep—" His words became mumbled as if someone had put a hand over his mouth.

"Come with me," the voice said again, and I realized it sounded like Maggie.

"Are you okay, Ali?" Alice asked quietly from beside me, and I heard one of the men behind us speak.

"Well, if she was going to pick you, she's not going to now." There was a lot of laughter.

"I'm okay, thank you."

"We were told that if we ran into you with him, to make sure he didn't speak to you."

"I appreciate that."

"You looked beautiful tonight," Maggie said and glanced back toward the corner that now stood vacant. "Sorry that we didn't tell you we were friends with him."

"Actually, I already knew you were. I saw you two talking to him after the first dance."

"You did?" Alice asked, surprised.

I nodded. "I did, and as much as I would love to talk now, I have to get to work."

"Work? It's after eight," Maggie said as I backed away from them.

"Yeah, I'm a chef. I work late. I have to go. It was great seeing you guys again."

I turned and rushed toward the taxi stand, waving my hand as one started to slow. Another moment and I was in the taxi, and we were zooming away. I glanced out the window and saw him standing at the corner, watching me go. Instinctively, I put my hand up to the glass as if I could touch him one last time.

I leaned back in my seat and gnawed on my lip. As much as I didn't want to consider Charlie's words, I thought she was right. Now I needed to figure out if I wanted safe or sexy.

CHAPTER SEVENTEEN

HARVEY

*W*e were heading out to eat dinner when I stepped ahead of the group and saw the flash of someone barreling around the corner. What was destiny trying to tell us here? This was the second time we had crashed into each other at a corner. Not just bumped into one another but crashed.

The first time, I was the one in a rush, now it was her turn. For that brief moment, I was tempted to take her face and kiss her again. I wanted to take up where we had left off, but Alice and Maggie were already pulling her away from me, and Greg clamped a hand over my mouth while Trevor yanked my arm toward the alley.

Jake laughed. "You know, I would have let you talk to her, but your sister scared me tonight when she said that she'd dip my man parts in hot oil if I let you two speak to one another."

"You're scared of Holly?" Trevor asked him.

"Wait, is Holly Melton's sister?" Joe jumped into the conversation.

"Duh!" Trevor said and knocked him upside the head.

"Damn, she was beautiful. You sure you don't want to introduce us?"

I glared at him. "Not on your life."

He shrugged, and then I turned to look back around the corner just in time to see her get into a taxi. She was wearing leggings, a sweatshirt, and sneakers and looked like she was heading out for a run. Was she racing to get away from us?

Alice and Maggie joined us again, and Maggie pointed at me. "You should be more careful."

"What? I didn't do anything. She's the one that came racing around the corner." I chuckled. "That's not the first time we have bumped into each other, either."

I proceeded to tell them about the night I went to Todd's and how I had run into her at another corner.

"Aww," Lexi said sweetly. "It's like it's meant to be."

Trevor laughed. "Two trains crashing in the night. Wonder how much carnage is going to come from it next time they meet?"

"Very funny," I growled at him. I turned to Maggie and Alice. "Did she say where she was rushing off to?"

"She was trying to get away from you," Wyatt joked, and I ignored him.

Alice and Maggie glanced at one another, and Alice shrugged. "She was on her way to work."

"Work? It's after eight."

"I guess she cooks someplace," Maggie said. "At least that's what she said as she left us."

She was a cook? Hmm, interesting. I wonder what she liked to cook. I turned back around and glanced down the road. What kind of restaurant did she work in? A tavern? A diner? Maybe one of those mom and pop places? Maybe at one of those franchised steak houses or Italian eateries. How many restaurants were there in the city? How long would it take me to visit each one to find her?

"Oh, geez," Alex sighed. "I can see his mind working now.

He's probably trying to figure out where she works so he can casually walk in and sit down."

I laughed. "I was not!"

Trevor shoved my arm. "Yes, you were."

I grinned. "Okay, I was."

"Just wait until Sunday, and then you'll know whether you made an impression on her or not."

"Fine," I growled. I hated waiting, but I didn't have much of a choice, now did I?

* * *

I WOKE up Sunday morning tense and pushed myself during my workout. I even ran a couple of extra miles just to try and wear off some of the anxiety—it didn't work. I was still a nervous wreck when I left the house to go to my meeting location.

Today was the day that I would find out if she chose me. I hoped that she did, and that wasn't just the competitor in me. I honestly did feel something with her, and I wanted to explore that. In fact, that's exactly what I told Tarin when I did my quickie interview before taking a seat at the coffee shop.

"What do you hope to achieve today?" Tarin asked me as we stood on the sidewalk.

"I hope that she shows up and that I finally get the opportunity to speak to her. I hope that we connected as well in person here on the street as we did on the dance floor. I'd love for this to work out for both of us."

"Well, go have a seat, and we'll see if she shows up."

I nervously took a seat and watched every person as they walked my direction. I'd never been so nervous before. A few minutes later, one of the employees stepped up to my table and handed me an envelope. I took it and glanced at the camera crew. Oddly enough, my sister was not here today, and I wondered where she was. That should have told me the answer.

I pulled open the envelope and read the words. "Thank you for the dance. I wish you all the best." I inhaled slowly and released it as I tapped the card on the table. "Wow. I thought she'd pick me."

"How are you feeling right now, Harvey?"

I stood and glanced down the street. "A little confused, I guess. I really thought we had something. I guess I was wrong."

"Are you disappointed?"

"Of course, I am."

"What are you going to do now?" the man asked.

"Now? Well, I'm going to go back to my job and keep doing what I do."

With that, someone said it's a wrap, and I shook their hands, thanked them for everything, and began to walk away. I guess my sister was with the other crew. I thought about calling her but decided against it.

Instead, I went home, grabbed a beer, plopped down on the couch, and turned on the television. My cellphone rang, and I saw Holly's name on it. I sent it to voicemail. A few minutes later, another number called, and I sent that one to voicemail. Then Greg called, and I thought that I better answer or the calls would keep coming in.

"Yeah," I said as I answered.

"Tough luck, my man. I'm sorry you didn't get chosen."

"How do you know that I didn't?"

"Because your sister called Maggie. She wanted to know if we'd spoken to you because you weren't answering her calls."

"Didn't feel like talking to anyone."

"Then why did you pick up for me?"

"Because I knew if I didn't, everyone and their fucking brother would have shown up here to check on me."

He laughed softly and then asked, "You alright?"

"Of course."

"Don't give me that shit. I know the guys were busting on

you, but you were really into the whole thing. I'm sure you are disappointed that she didn't choose you."

"I am."

"Yeah, well, you can mope around today, but tomorrow, make sure all your makeup is put away, and you have your guns strapped on. You are back in class."

I laughed. "Yeah, no more makeup for me. I'll see you tomorrow."

"She doesn't know what she's missing," Greg said. "Or maybe she heard about those damn green shakes you drink, and it turned her off."

"You're an ass," I hissed at him but laughed after. "I'll talk at you later."

"You got it."

After I hung up, I sat there and thought back over the whole thing. How had I been so wrong? I really thought that we had something together. I couldn't picture her with the other guy.

I was on my third beer when I heard my front door open, and I rolled my eyes. Damn, I forgot Holly had a key. Her heels made clipping sounds on the hard tile floor as she came back toward the family room.

"Why aren't you answering my calls?"

"Did you call? I was watching the game."

She smacked the top of my head. "You're pissed at me because she didn't pick you."

I sat up and swung my feet to the floor, finishing the beer in my hand and then getting up to get another. "I'm not pissed at anyone. I only did that whole thing as a favor to you. It meant nothing."

"Oh, bullshit, Harvey. You liked her. I'm sorry that she chose Blake."

"Blake? Figures his name is something like Blake." I sat back down, tipping the bottle to my mouth again.

"Oh, stop being petty, it does not suit you. To be completely honest, most of us were shocked that she chose Blake. I know I was."

I turned and looked at my sister. She looked like she was telling the truth. "You thought she would pick me?"

"Yes, I did. I hoped that she would pick you."

"I thought you said I wasn't her type."

"You aren't her normal type, but that's why I wanted you on the show. I knew that she would like you. I was hoping she would take a chance and pick you."

I squinted at her. "Was there ever a guy who broke his leg?" She winced ever so slightly. "Holy shit, Holly. This was a setup from the beginning."

"Yeah, I'm sorry, Harv."

"Why the hell would you do that, Holly?"

"Because I wanted you to find someone good. She is fantastic, and I could see you with her. I was hoping that she would see it too."

"How well do you know her?"

"I know Ali really well. We've been friends for a while."

I paused—Ali—it was a pretty name for her. "I can't believe this was a setup. That's why you told me to burn my time at work. You even helped me pick out the dates." I paused. "Wait! Did you talk to Jake about it? He was pushing me to take time off too."

"Yeah, I kind of did."

"Jesus, Holly. I can't believe you did that."

"Harvey, don't be mad. I was trying to help you."

"Holly, do you like it when I get in your personal business with the men you date? No, you don't, so why would you think it would be alright for you to barge into mine? That was a pretty crappy thing to do."

"I'm sorry, Harvey. I honestly did think that she was going to pick you. When I found out, I was shocked. I even asked her if she was serious, and she said—"

I stared at my sister. "What did she say?"

She sighed and closed her eyes for a moment, wiping her hands over her head before she looked at me and answered. "She said that she needed safe, not sexy in her life right now."

"Safe? He made her feel safe? That guy looked like a fruitcake."

"I think she meant more along the lines of he was a safer choice, that she didn't expect any surprises from him."

"That's bullshit." I was pissed, that woman—Ali—didn't have any idea what kind of man I was, or how protected and safe she would have been with me.

"I'm sorry, Harvey."

I put my hand up. "I know you are, Holly, but can you just let it go? I don't want to know anything else about her. Just stop talking about her. I wish her the best, now let's move on."

Holly sighed. "Fine, I'll let it go, but for the record, she would have been perfect for you."

I glared at her. She got up and went into the kitchen to get a beer for herself. When she returned, she asked, "What's the score?"

CHAPTER EIGHTEEN

ALI

*T*he decision weighed heavily on my mind day and night on Saturday. Even amid Saturday night rush hour in the kitchen, my mind continually wrestled with the decision.

There was this massive piece of me that wanted to pick dancer one, just because I knew it would be stimulating and undoubtedly fun. However, the practical side of me said to choose dancer two. He didn't make my heart flutter when he looked into my eyes, but he had a beautiful smile that I did not doubt reached right into his heart.

On Saturday afternoon, Charlie and I had gone to Holly's office, and we'd gotten to see all four dances. This was the first time that I had seen myself in action, and after watching them, I was more torn than I had been before—at least for a little while.

Dancing with the second guy had been easy, and we looked striking as a couple. He was big; I was tiny. He was light, and I was dark. He moved with purpose, and I traveled with a grace that I would never have thought myself capable of.

The dances with the first man were incredible to watch. He brought something out in me, something that almost scared me.

He wasn't much bigger than me, and yet he had lifted and held me with more strength than the other man. When our bodies came together, our hair blended, and our torsos fit against one another's so entirely. It was as if we were made for one another.

That thought scared me. Not because I thought we fit so perfectly together, but because I saw something different in myself as I watched the two of us dance. I saw a fierceness, a willingness to throw caution to the wind, and that was not who I was.

I was structure.

I was careful.

I was a woman who thought before she did anything and made sure she weighed every risk before doing it.

I would never admit this to anyone—but I wanted to be the other woman—she scared and excited me—almost as much as he did.

As I watched the romantic dance with my first partner, my heart clenched in my chest. Charlie was right; he did seem lost as I walked away. Would I be lost without him if I chose him, and then it did not work?

That specific thought is how I based my decision. I could not afford to be lost. I could not afford to take that kind of chance right now. My life was too busy, and while I was right where I wanted to be, I still had plans. One day I would own my own restaurant. Dancer one could pull me from my dreams, and I couldn't afford for that to happen.

I didn't tell Charlie what I had decided. I let her go on and on about the two men. Holly was quiet as we left her office. It looked as if she wanted to say something, but knew she shouldn't.

On Sunday, Holly showed up at my door with two camera crews. I handed her my envelope. "For dancer one."

Holly seemed shocked. "Are you sure, Ali?"

"I need safe, not sexy. I'm sure."

A sadness came over her eyes, but she blinked it away quickly. "Okay then. Let's go meet dancer number two."

She handed the envelope off to one of the crew members, shaking her head slightly. I watched the van pull away from the curb as I got into my car to follow Holly to the location I would meet my date.

Holly and a smaller third crew were with me around the corner from the small outdoor café. I was nervous but excited. I tried not to think about what the other man would be going through.

I turned to Holly abruptly. "What was his name?" She raised a brow as if confused. "Dancer one. What was his name?"

She smiled sadly. "His name is Harvey; they call him Harv."

"Harvey," I nodded. I hadn't pictured that name for him, but I liked it. It was a strong, masculine name. "Thank you."

"You're welcome." She spoke with a few people, and then turned to me. "Okay, you ready? He's waiting for you."

I blew out a burst of air and rolled my shoulders. "Yeah, I'm ready."

Tarin came on camera with me and asked me a few questions about being nervous and how hard the decision was. When I thought back on the process, it wasn't all that hard. The hardest part was reminding myself that I wanted safe, not the unknown.

We finished the interview questions, and then I walked around the corner and toward the small café seating area. There was a camera on him, but I knew by the angle that it was picking me up too. I was both excited and a little nervous as I stepped around him.

"Hi," I said with more bubble in my voice than expected. His eyes snapped to mine, and a wide grin spread over his features as he quickly came to his feet.

"Wow, I hoped you'd pick me, but I was worried you wouldn't." He put his hand out. "I'm Blake Monahan."

I shook his hand. "Ali Davidson," I replied.

"Can I give you a hug?" he suddenly asked, and I grinned up at him and stepped forward. The hug was lovely, and for only a brief moment, I thought about the fact that it didn't make me tingle. I didn't need tingle; I needed reliable.

"Have a seat." He held my chair out for me. "Wow, I can't believe this. What a ride this has been, huh?"

"Yes, it has been crazy."

"That last dance we did, I wasn't sure I'd be able to learn it."

"You?" I laughed as a drink was put down in front of me. "I was the one that had to learn all those in the air things."

He chuckled, and I smiled. I liked the sound of his voice and his laugh. "So, what do you do, Ali? Are you a professional dancer?"

I threw my head back and laughed. "Oh, god! No! Normally, I can't even dance at all. Not sure what came over me during the last two weeks, but don't depend on that." I smiled at him, feeling very comfortable. "I'm a chef."

"What? Like you like to cook?"

"Yes, I love to cook, but I'm a Head Chef at Randolph's French Restaurant. Do you like to cook?"

He snickered. "I have issues boiling water." At least he admitted it, and I wouldn't have to deal with him cooking in the kitchen. "You are welcome to cook for me anytime, although you don't have to cook." He backpedaled as if he wasn't sure he should have said that.

"It's okay; I enjoy cooking. I'd love to cook for you some-time. What do you do?"

"I work in finance."

"Finance?"

"Yeah, I manage a bank."

Well, you couldn't get more stable and reliable than that, now could you? The two of us finished our drinks and took a walk in the nearby park. The camera crew followed us for a little while, then quietly disappeared. I enjoyed my conversation with Blake and honestly felt that I had made the right decision.

At the end of our time, we traded phone numbers and made a date for lunch later in the week. Our schedules were going to be a little tough to work around, but if it was meant to be, it would work itself out. I felt good about my decision, and as I caught a ride to the restaurant, I returned the phone call to Charlie.

"So is he as sexy in person as he was on camera?"

"I didn't pick Harvey."

"Harvey? That was his name? Wait! You picked the blond guy? Why?" she cried over the phone.

"Because I needed safe, not sexy in my life, Charlie. You know I don't have time for a crazy romance. I need to find someone who can slip into my world and not make waves. Harvey looked like he would have brought along hurricane-sized waves."

"Oh, my god! Have I not taught you anything? Damn, Ali! You should have gone for the sex! Just once, you should have listened to me!"

"Blake is really nice. I think we are going to be able to build a nice relationship. You're going to like him."

"Blake? He sounds like a surfer dude. What does he do?"

"He manages a bank."

"Bor-ing! Holy smokes, Ali. I can't believe you picked Mr. Safe. You are going to regret it."

"No, I'm not. Charlie, can't you just be happy for me? He's a really nice guy, and I know that we are going to get along really well."

She sighed. "Fine, I'll support you because you are my best friend, but I still think you chose wrong. How did you find out what his name was?"

"I asked Holly."

"What's his last name?"

"Why?"

"Because I want to look him up. You might not be interested, but I sure am. Besides, I'd love to see him move from behind the camera."

"You stay away from him, Charlie!" I hissed at her.

"Why? You don't want him. Why can't I have him? It's not like you two slept together, and it's messy seconds. You danced with the guy a couple of times."

I closed my eyes, rubbing my temples. "Fine, whatever. I'll give you Holly's phone number, and you can call her yourself."

"You don't want to do it for me?"

"I don't want to know any more about him than I already do."

"Yeah, why not? Afraid you are going to regret your decision?"

"No!" I snapped. "I am not going to regret my decision. I like Blake. He is exactly the type of man that I was looking for. I know that things between us will be great. You just wait and see."

"Yeah, okay. You tell me how great things are in eight weeks when your episode goes on air. Let's see if you two are still together or not."

"I do not doubt that we will be together, Charlie. It feels right. I know I made the right choice."

CHAPTER NINETEEN

HARVEY

Seven Weeks Later

"How ow was the flight back?" Jake asked as I took a seat in his office.

"Better than the flight out. I wasn't sure we'd make it there in one piece. There were a few times I wanted to beg the pilot to turn around."

"Yeah, I'm surprised they wanted to fly with that storm off the coast, but I'm glad you all got over there safely."

"I think all of us were a little airsick by the time we got to the other side of the turbulence." I chuckled. "Although Maggie seemed to be the best out of all of us."

"How did she do with the rest of it?"

"That woman is a freaking trooper. She just kept on going; in fact, she was showing Wyatt up left and right. Every time he whined, she'd jump down his throat and tell him to suck it up and stop whining."

Jake laughed as someone stepped into the room behind us. "Hey, welcome back," Alex said as he clapped my back.

"Thanks," I told him as he took a seat.

"I was just telling Jake how awesome Maggie was. I'm serious; I will travel with that woman anywhere. She's got bigger balls than most men."

Alex chuckled. "Probably not a wise thing to say to Greg."

"Dude, who do you think put that thought into my head. He told me he's scared of her half the time, and the other half amazed at how she just blazes through. The woman is a tough nut, not just a pretty face."

"Too bad we don't have more of those around. We could use a few more tough women," Jake said.

"You know Alice could give you a run for your money," I replied, and Jake turned away as if the thought bored him. "I'm serious. You should consider letting her off the desk. I'm sure she would be awesome out in the field. She deserves better than being an administrative assistant."

"There is no way I would let Alice go overseas. She'd get hurt."

Alex and I laughed. "You aren't worried that Maggie will get hurt?"

"She's got Greg to watch out for her," he snapped back. "And obviously, you too."

"You could watch out for Alice."

Alex shook his head. "Alice doesn't need either of you to watch out for her."

"Can we stop talking about Alice?" Jake growled. "She has nothing to do with this. What else happened on the delivery?"

For another few minutes, I shared more of our trip, and then Alice showed up in the office and said she needed to speak with Jake privately. I shot her a wink as I left the office.

A few minutes later, I was being called back to the office again. "What's up?"

"I need you to handle a situation," Jake said.

"What situation?" I glanced between Jake and Alice for a

moment. She gave me a sly smile that I did not understand in the least bit.

"A friend needs some help with some security."

"Okay—" I said slowly, waiting for more.

"Get with Mike and go check the place out. They need some specialized cameras."

"Why do you need me? Can't Mike do it on his own? He is the tech guy."

"Because I want you to go too," he hissed and then glared at Alice for a moment. She smiled sweetly at him, and he rolled his eyes.

"Just go check it out, see what they might need, and get it set up."

"What is this about? I mean, what's going on?"

"You'll find out when you get there. I don't know the details, and I don't fucking want to know either."

"Then why are we doing this?"

"Because I'm doing Alice a favor." He stared at her, and she widened her smile.

"You can thank me later." She patted me on the chest as she walked out of the room.

"Thank her later? For what?"

"I don't know. Just go take care of it, or she's going to drive me nuts."

"Alice drives you nuts anyway. The two of you need to sleep together already."

"I have no desire to sleep with Alice."

I barked out a laugh. "Yeah, okay, boss. Keep telling yourself that," I muttered as I left his office.

I grabbed Mike, told him what I knew, which wasn't much, and then stopped at Alice's desk. "So, what is going on?"

"I have a friend who needs help. She thinks someone might be sabotaging her business, and she wants cameras installed to watch the employees."

"Why doesn't she just hire a security company to do that?"

Alice gave me her signature, aren't you just so cute and dumb look. "We are a security company. She needs this done quietly, without anyone else knowing."

"Alright, where are we going?" Mike asked. Alice gave us an address, and we headed out.

"Randolph's," Mike said, "huh, fancy place. You ever eaten there?"

"Nah, too rich for my blood. Not the kind of place I go to when I want to kick back. That's the kind of restaurant you'd go to impress someone."

"Yeah, no wonder I have never been there. No one to impress."

I chuckled from behind the wheel. "Yeah, me either."

Maybe if Ali had chosen me, I would have splurged for such a meal, or perhaps not. She didn't strike me as the elegant dining type of woman. Not that I really knew what kind of a woman she was.

Ever since my last conversation with Holly, I hadn't spoken about it to anyone. Not even the guys, or Alice and Maggie. Everyone had let it go, and I appreciated it. From time to time, when I heard the song on the radio that we'd danced to, I would think about her and hoped that she was doing well with the other guy.

I knew that the show would be airing on television soon, and I was still on the fence about watching it or not. Maybe I would, or maybe I wouldn't. I guess that would depend on how I felt that day, and if I wanted to have it rubbed in my face.

I growled silently to myself as we pulled down an alley and parked behind the restaurant as requested. Mike carried a notebook and was at the back door to the kitchen before me.

He knocked, and it opened a moment later. I was looking down at my phone when the door opened, and I started to step forward to introduce myself. I glanced up and did a double take as the woman gasped. "You!"

"Um," I hesitated. I could turn around and walk the fuck away, or I could man up and be a professional here. So she hadn't picked me; she went with someone else. I needed to get over that. "Hi, I didn't expect to see you again. I'm Harvey, and this is Mike. We work with Safety Zone Security. I think you were expecting us."

She laughed, slightly uncomfortable, or maybe nervously. "Hi, Harvey, Mike. I'm Ali Davidson; please come in."

She stepped to the side, looking away from me and biting her lip. Holy shit! Alice had known about this! Did Jake? Is that why Jake hadn't said anything? What the hell!

"What's the sitrep here?" Mike asked as he leaned toward me and spoke softly. "Anything I should know?"

I shook my head slightly and turned to Ali. Her dark hair was pulled back in a ponytail at the base of her neck, and she wore chef pants and a t-shirt with black sneakers. She looked so different than when we had danced but just as good—if not better.

"Um…" She swallowed nervously as her eyes jumped everywhere but toward me. "Did Alice explain what was going on?"

"No," Mike said after I didn't answer. She glanced at me and then turned her gaze to him. I figured it would probably be easier for her to speak with him. In fact, it would probably be a whole lot easier on both of us if I wasn't even here. Why the hell would they do this to me? "We only know that something is going on here, and you needed some cameras."

"Okay, so, about two months ago, I had an issue with food poisoning here in the kitchen."

"You had food poisoning?" I asked, and she shook her head, keeping her attention on Mike.

"No, a customer, actually two."

"Alright, what does that have to do with someone sabotaging your business?" He glanced around. "Is this your restaurant?"

"No, not really. I'm the Head Chef here, so while I don't own it, it's my restaurant because I run it. I control everything that happens in my kitchen. The Health Department came out and inspected our kitchen twice then, once they closed us for two days, but everything came back clean. All the tests were normal. I demand my employees to keep the highest of cleaning standards."

"So maybe they got it from someplace else," Mike replied.

"I would like to think so, but my kitchen is the only constant."

"So if this happened two months ago, why are you asking for help now?" he asked her.

"Because last week there was another case, and yesterday, there were two more." She winced, and her gaze fell on mine. I saw the frustration and pain in her eyes, but more than that, I saw anger and the need to fight back. "If I don't figure out what is going on, they are going to close my kitchen down for good. I'll be ruined as a chef. I can't afford that, especially when I am not doing anything wrong."

"So, you want us to put cameras in your kitchen because you think one of your employees is responsible for poisoning the diners?"

"I hate to think that, but it's the only thing I can come up with." She crossed her arms over her chest, looking uncomfortable, and then she dropped them. "It has to be someone in my kitchen. The Health Department has me on their shit list now, excuse my French, and they are determined to find something and pin it on me so they can fine the hell out of me and shut down this kitchen. I am not going down without a fight. I refuse to have someone think I have a dirty kitchen when it is anything but."

I glanced around and saw nothing but spotless work areas

and neatly stacked cooking equipment. Mike was doing the same thing. "Okay, so tell us how many people work here?"

"There are twelve of us here in the main kitchen."

"Thirteen? You oversee twelve people?" I asked, and she hiked a brow.

"Yes, twelve. Why does that surprise you?"

"I'm just surprised that there are so many people that work in the kitchen. That was nothing against you, Ms. Davidson."

She paused and swallowed. "I'm sorry. That was uncalled for."

"Don't worry about it," I said. She had the right to be defensive, especially if someone was out to get her.

"Tell us about the people in the kitchen." Mike urged her and then paused. "You don't mind if I record this, do you? I know some people are camera shy, but it will give us a chance to look back over it after this and decide the best locations to put them."

She looked at me. "I think I got over being camera shy a few weeks ago. Do what you need to do." Mike gave me a questioning look but then turned on his recorder on his phone as she walked us around the area, pointing out what area was for what and who takes care of it.

"Do you have a measuring tape?" Mike asked her, and she shook her head.

"Sorry I don't think so."

"I have one in my console," I told Mike and started to head toward the door, but he grabbed my arm and held his hand out.

"I'll get it, just give me your keys."

I almost told him that I'd do it, but at the last second, I handed him the key fob. Both Ali and I watched him leave, and I wondered if I was the only one to feel the tension building around us.

The door closed, and we both continued to stare at it. I finally cleared my throat. "You did a really good job with the dances. I hope you enjoyed yourself."

She turned to me, a look of thankfulness on her features. As if she had been afraid to bring it up and was glad that I had. "Thank you, and you did too." She gnawed on her bottom lip for a moment.

"It was fun."

"It was," she commented quietly and then lifted her green eyes to mine. "I'm sorry."

Oh, the temptation to reach out and touch her was so strong. I shoved my hands into my pockets instead. "Hey, you had to do what you felt was right. I hope safe is working out for you." Her lips parted in surprise, and I wanted to knock myself out for saying that. What an ass I was! I put my hand up. "I'm sorry. That was rude, but I do hope that you two are doing well and you are happy. Look, I'm going to go see what is taking him so long. I'll make sure that someone else comes back to help Mike so that you don't have to see me again. I don't want to make you uncomfortable."

I rushed away from her before she could say a word, the entire time kicking myself in the ass. When I stepped outside, I found Mike leaning against the truck.

"What are you doing?"

"That didn't take long."

"What didn't take long?"

"For you to run away."

"What the fuck are you talking about?"

"Dude, I put two and two together. Both of you were acting strange, and when she mentioned being used to the cameras, I figured it out. She's the one that you danced with on that show, isn't she?"

"Yeah, so?"

He laughed as he pushed off the truck. "She's also the one that twisted your head around your heart. I was hoping if I gave you two a few minutes, you could get yourself straightened out."

"There is nothing to straighten out. She picked the other guy."

"Yeah, but I'm pretty sure after seeing the way she was watching you, that she sure wished that she hadn't."

"Whatever! Man, just go in there and do what you need to do. I'm going to wait out here in the truck."

He chuckled as he headed toward the door. "Don't say I didn't try to help."

"Ass," I muttered as I opened my door and climbed in.

CHAPTER TWENTY

ALI

"*I* have no clue what the hell to do now," I muttered, and Charlie patted my back, while Holly pushed my drink closer. "I swear someone is out to get me."

"What makes you think that?" Holly asked.

"Because Ali's being a drama queen," Charlie replied to Holly, and I glared at her.

"I am not being a drama queen, Char. Someone is poisoning my partons, and I don't know who."

"Are you sure it's a person and not a circumstance?"

"It has to be a person!" I smacked my hand down on the bar hard enough to hurt. "It is not possible to get random E. coli poisonings like this. None of these people have eaten the same thing. None of them have even been to the restaurant at the same time. It doesn't make sense." I rubbed my hands over my face.

"What can we do to help?" Holly asked.

"Do you know anyone who knows anything about putting hidden cameras around a kitchen? Because other than that, I'm not sure what the hell to do."

"Actually, I do," Holly replied with a grin.

"Really?" I asked, surprised, and she nodded.

"Let me make a phone call." She grabbed her phone and slipped off her barstool, heading to the door where it was quieter.

"How long are you closed now?"

"Two days. Two freaking days," I growled as I tossed my hands into the air.

"Maybe you should give Blake a call now that you have time off."

"No, I officially broke it off with him."

Her brows popped, and then she smiled. "You did?"

"Why do you look so damn happy about that?"

She ignored my question. "Why did you break it off? I thought you liked him."

"I did like him, but he had an issue with the fact that I always worked at night. He started hinting about me finding a different job where I could work during the day, and I would be able to cook for him at night."

Charlie chuckled as Holly came back to her seat. "I am going to have someone come to see you tomorrow."

"You are?"

"Yep! They need to take a look at the kitchen and figure out how many they will need, but they will be able to put cameras up and monitor them for you."

"That's fantastic!" I said, then tugged my bottom lip under my teeth. "Is it wrong to do this?"

"No," Charlie immediately commented, and Holly kind of winced as Charlie continued. "Hey, someone is trying to hurt people. She's not spying on her peeps to catch them sneaking food. Ali needs to know who is poisoning these people."

"Yes, that's true. Maybe you can put up one or two visible cameras. You could say the insurance company is requiring it as the policy is updating or something."

I nodded as I thought about that. "That's a good idea. I could do that. I could put two primary cameras in the kitchen and one at the back entrance for safety. I don't have to tell them about the hidden ones."

"Just don't record sound, and you should be alright. You know you need to have permission to record sound."

"I could make everyone aware that the cameras are in the kitchen and get consent. They don't need to know about the smaller ones, but permission would allow me to record sound."

"That would work," Charlie said. "See, we figured it out! Now let's get back to why you broke it off with Blake."

"Ah, you told her." Holly laughed as she sipped her drink.

"How did Holly know already?"

"I had to tell her because they were getting ready to do the update on us for the show. It airs this weekend."

"I bet you would have had better luck with Mr. Sexy. What was his name?"

"Harvey," Holly and I responded at the same time and then laughed. I hated to admit it, but I had thought about Mr. Sexy more times than I cared to admit.

"I agree, I think she would have done better with him."

"How do you guys know that?"

Holly studied me for a moment. "Remember, I told you that one of the contestants had broken his leg?"

"Yes, and you got someone to fill in for him."

"Yeah, I lied," Holly smirked. "I totally thought you would like Harvey. In fact, I thought you two would be perfect together."

"What made you think that we would be good for one another?" I put my hand up. "Wait, did he know you lied about that contestant being hurt?"

"Not until it was over. I lied to Harvey too."

"Did he forgive you?" I asked, spiking a brow at her.

"Yeah," she muttered, but then laughed. "He did. But he had to."

"Why?"

"Because he's family, Ali. Harvey is my brother."

My jaw dropped. "Your brother? Harvey is your brother? You tried to set me up with your brother, Holly? Without telling me! Oh, my god! Wait, isn't he in the military?"

"No, he was in the military. He's retired now."

"I can't believe you lied to both of us." I shook my head as Charlie leaned around me.

"Your brother is hot. Is he still single?"

"As far as I know, he is, but he's out of town right now."

"What does he do now?"

Holly shook her head and looked around the bar. "I don't know exactly. I just know he travels a lot."

"Find out if he is single and let me know," Charlie said. "You don't mind, do you, Ali?"

Oh, I minded, but I wasn't going to say that to her. Instead, I smiled. "Nope, not at all."

Charlie laughed. "She just lied to me. She wants to stab me in the eye right now."

"I do not!" I hissed.

"You smiled, showing your teeth. Anytime you do that, you're lying!"

Holly broke out in hysterics, and I started to giggle too. "Okay, I did lie. Stay away from him, at least for a little while longer."

Charlie squeezed my forearm. "I will. I was just trying to get a rise out of you." Then she mouthed to Holly that she really did want his number. I rolled my eyes at her.

* * *

THE NEXT MORNING, I was at the restaurant by nine and staring at the kitchen. I hated that people were getting sick here, and I was so frustrated from dealing with the Health Department.

One of their employees, I think his name was Jack, said something to me on the side when nasty Henry Marks was busy. What he suggested had planted the seed that someone was doing this on purpose. Why else would there not be any signs of it?

When I heard a knock on the back door, I quickly opened it to see a tall man standing there, smiling, and then he moved. My world shifted, and I was glad that I was holding on to the door, or I would have stumbled back and fallen. "You!"

"Um," he hesitated, "hi, I didn't expect to see you again. I'm Harvey, and this is Mike. We work with Safety Zone Security. I think you were expecting us."

I sure as hell wasn't expecting him. Oh, Holly was in so much trouble! She had lied to me—again! Traveling my ass! She knew exactly what he did for a living. I had a mind to call her right now, but I didn't. I'd wait till they left and then give her an earful!

Somehow I kept it together and didn't freak out and fawn all over him. Both Charlie and Holly had been right. I should have gone with him, but I had wanted safe. What an idiot I was.

Safe turned out to be slightly dull, and then dull turned into nagging because he worked days, I worked nights, blah, blah, blah. It was the same argument—a different man. When Blake asked if I wanted kids, and if I planned to stay home to raise them, flags had begun waving like the Fourth of July, and I immediately told him that I didn't think things would work for us. Yes, he was handsome, and he was kind, and I did like him. We had some chemistry, and our few makeout sessions were exciting, but they still didn't make me tingle. I wanted to tingle.

The man standing a few feet away from me could make me tingle. He could probably make me scream or drop to my knees and beg, but that wasn't going to happen. I had to stop thinking about him in any other capacity other than his job.

That was easy enough to do—sort of—while I talked about

work, but the minute that Mike left us alone, I wanted to flee or grab him and kiss him and see if he made my body tingle again. Would that be wrong? I was totally at a loss for words and thankful that he spoke.

"You did a really good job with the dances. I hope you enjoyed yourself."

"Thank you, and you did too." The temptation to blurt out that I had chosen wrong was so strong that I don't know how I held them back.

"It was fun."

"It was," I told him, and then looked him in the eye. The least I could do was apologize. "I'm sorry."

For a second, I thought he would approach me. God, how I wanted him to, but instead, he stepped back. "Hey, you had to do what you felt was right. I hope safe is working out for you."

What? What did he know about safe? Had Holly told him what I said? Oh, my god! She did!

"I'm sorry. That was rude, but I do hope that you two are doing well and you are happy. Look, I'm going to go see what is taking him so long. I'll make sure that someone else comes back to help Mike so that you don't have to see me again. I don't want to make you uncomfortable."

I watched him leave. Oh, Holly Melton, wait till I get my hands on you! I put my face into my hands and sighed. A moment later, the door opened, and I jerked my head up, expecting to see Harvey, but it was only Mike.

"I need to take a few measurements. You don't mind, do you?"

"No, do anything that you need to do."

He started to take measurements and looked around, jotting notes on a pad. "Don't mind, Melton. He was a little broken-hearted when you picked the other guy."

"Did he tell you that?"

Mike chuckled. "No, he didn't need to. He refused to talk

about it at all. That's not him. When he's upset, he shuts stuff down."

"How well do you know him?"

"He's like a brother." He grinned toward me. "And that's why I'll say this. If things don't work out with that other guy, let Harv know. He is a good man."

"Thank you," I replied. I wasn't ready to mention to Mike that I wasn't with the other guy anymore. The world would know soon enough. In fact, only three more days, and everyone would know that I had chosen wrong.

I waited while he did what he needed, then Mike explained that he would need to get the right cameras and would need several hours to put them into position. We discussed an approximate date and decided that Friday night after the restaurant was closed—if we were able to open at all—I could meet them here, and they could set it all up.

Mike explained that he would have a couple of guys with him and then paused. "If having Harvey around is going to be a problem, you let me know. I'll have someone else come."

"No, it won't be a problem for me, but if he's not comfortable, don't make him or give him a hard time about it. I don't want to upset him."

He laughed. "You're nicer than I would be. I'll give you a shout in a day or so to let you know that we are a go."

"Sounds good, thanks, Mike."

As I showed him out, I stood at the door and locked eyes with Harvey, who sat behind the steering wheel in the pickup. He lifted his fingers off the wheel and waved. I waved back, and then slowly closed the door.

I pulled my phone out of my pocket and called Holly. It went to voicemail, and I growled after the beep. "You lied to me again! Holly Melton, if you don't stop lying to me, I'm not going to be your friend anymore, and there will be no more decadent midnight mousse for you!"

I set the phone down and then replayed the whole scene over again. He really was a handsome man who exuded strength and power—and sex. It wasn't that he was large or overbearing; it was the way he looked at you like he wanted to devour you—I shivered. My god, I wanted that. Why did I ever think safe was the way to go?

CHAPTER TWENTY-ONE

HARVEY

*E*ven though I was furious, I knew it wasn't Mike's fault. The two of us discussed the number of cameras and positions that would be best for the kitchen. He decided that unless stations were really close, each one should have a specific camera, and then several other blind locations would need eyes. We decided that we wanted every inch of the room covered. If we were going to do this, we were going to do it right.

When we got back to the office, I was on a mission as I exited the elevator. Alice must have seen me coming because she was out of her seat and disappeared around the corner as I opened the front door. "Alice!"

There was no way that she didn't hear me, but that didn't stop her. I heard a door close down the hall and knew she had just locked herself into the bathroom. I headed toward Jake's office and burst inside to find Trevor and Maggie sitting across from him.

He spiked a brow. "You got a problem, Melt-man?"

"Yeah, I got a problem. I do not appreciate being blindsided. Did you know who we were going to see?"

"Why does it matter who it is? Aren't you professional enough to do your fucking job?"

"Of course, I'm a professional, but I was less of one today because I was fucking blindsided. You should have said something. What if I did that shit to you, Jake?"

"Then I would have fired you."

"Yes, well, I can't do that, now can I?"

"What did you do?" Maggie asked as she continued to ping pong between the two of us.

"I sent him out on a local job," Jake replied dryly.

"No, him and Alice." I pointed over my shoulder. "And I know it is her that really set this shit up—sent me over to Randolph's to help Ali Davidson with an issue."

Maggie started grinning. "Oh, really?"

I growled at her. "This is not funny, Maggie."

"Who is Ali Davidson?" Trevor asked, completely lost.

Maggie turned to him and put her hand on his wrist. "That's the woman he danced with."

Trevor smirked. "You mean the one that turned him down?"

"Shut up, Vaughn."

Maggie got up and came to me. "What did she say?"

"Maggie, this was not a date; this was work."

"Are you going to help her with something?"

"Yeah, I am." I forced myself to calm down. "Of course, I am, but I don't appreciate being surprised like that. You all could have warned me, and then I wouldn't have looked like such an idiot."

"Oh, I'm sure you didn't look like an idiot."

Mike spoke from behind me, near the door. "He acted like an ass."

"Sometimes, I really fucking hate you guys," I muttered as I put my hands on my hips and hung my head.

Maggie rubbed my arm. "I'm sure it wasn't that bad."

My laugh sounded strangled. "No, it was pretty bad."

Mike jumped in. "Yeah, but he can make it up to her. We are going to need four visual cameras, eleven stainless-steel minis, and nine mini whites."

"Jesus, how big is the kitchen?" Jake asked.

"It's pretty big," he answered.

"She believes one of the employees might be doing something to the food. She's got twelve direct employees in the kitchen, so we wanted every spot covered, plus some of the areas where other restaurant staff have access to the food."

"When are you going to set it up?" Trevor asked.

"Friday night," Mike replied.

"Damn, sorry, I would help, but Davina and I are heading out of town for the weekend."

"Are you and Greg around this weekend?" I asked Maggie.

She shook her head. "No, we borrowed Mike's cabin for the weekend." She smiled at Mike. "We are leaving Friday right after work."

"Okay, so that leaves Harv, Alex, and me to get it done." Mike looked at Jake. "Unless you want to join us."

"Nah, you guys can take care of it. I have plans."

Mike glanced at me and shrugged. "It won't take that long; the three of us can knock it out in a few hours."

"Yeah, I'm sure," I commented.

I turned to head out of the office, and Maggie grabbed hold of my arm. "How was she?"

"Who?" I knew who she was asking about, but I didn't want her to know the mess my head was.

"Don't give me that crap, Melt-man—by the way, that's a weird nickname." Maggie laughed.

I chuckled. "Jake gave it to me years ago. She was okay. Surprised to see me, and uncomfortable too. She did say she was sorry."

"She did? For what?"

I scratched the side of my face. "Yeah, I'm not sure what the apology was for exactly because I spouted off about it not being a big deal and walked out."

"Harvey! That's wasn't very nice."

"No, not my finest moment. I'll apologize to her on Friday when I see her again. At least this time, I'll be prepared to see her."

"Is that going to help?"

"Pft—easy peasy."

* * *

FRIDAY NIGHT—SCRATCH that—very early Saturday morning, Alex and I sat down the street and waited for the last employee to leave. At twelve thirty-four, Alex's phone pinged.

"Coast is clear."

I started the truck, and we headed down the alley. I had told Maggie that this would be easy, but seeing Ali standing at the back door was like a punch to the solar plexus.

Alex laughed when I made a groaning noise. "You okay over there?"

"Yeah, man. I just need to keep my shit straight, and my mouth closed and get this done."

Alex glanced out the window. "She's a very pretty woman."

"She is."

Alex turned to me as he grabbed the door handle. "Don't count her out yet. You met her for a reason; you might not have found out what the reason is yet." He grinned. "Hey, I never would have expected a package delivered to the wrong apart-ment would have led me to Lexi."

"True."

"You're back here for a reason; keep an open mind as to what that could be."

"Let's just get this job done, Romeo."

He chuckled as we got out of the truck, and I saw Ali brush

her hair back from her face and shift on her feet. Was she as nervous as I was?

"Evening, Ms. Davidson. This is Alex Miller. Mike got called away on another job."

"Ali, please call me Ali." She put her hand out to Alex, and he shook it.

"I'm going to show him where things are going to go, and then we will bring in the gear. Is that a problem?"

She shook her head. "No, do what you need to do. I'll be in my office."

I nodded at her as she passed by, getting a whiff of multiple scents on her as she passed. I guess as a chef, she would have a lot of smells on her clothes. It almost made me hungry. Although part of my hunger would be to get her undressed and under me. Shit! I needed to forget about that and focus. She had chosen someone else.

I explained where things would go to Alex, and then we unloaded the truck. Alex and I joked about work on and off as we started setting things up. We worked on the wiring for the visible cameras that the employees would be aware of, and then set up the extra router and booster that we'd need to keep the signal strong enough for all the other wi-fi minis.

Just after we had the main wiring down, Alex got a call. "Why are you up?" He climbed down the ladder he was on and looked at me. "Are you okay?" He was quiet for a moment. "Alright, I'll be right there. Stay calm."

"What's up?"

He hung up the phone. "Give me your keys."

"What?"

"Lexi isn't feeling well. I have to get home."

"Shit!" I tossed him the keys. "Go, man!"

He started to leave and then looked at all our gear. "What about—"

"Don't worry about it; I'll call Jake and get his ass up to come to get me. Go! Take care of Lex."

Alex's face was tense as he turned and rushed for the door. A few seconds later, Ali popped her head into the kitchen. "Where did Alex go?"

"Um..." Holy crap! Ali and I were now alone. Breathe, man, just breathe. "His wife is pregnant. He just got a call that she wasn't feeling well." I turned away and started busying myself. Although I had no clue what I was doing because the only thing I could think about was that I was alone with her.

"Oh, I hope she is okay."

"Yeah, me too." I put my hands on my hips and sighed as I stared at the gear. "This is going to take longer with just me doing it. I'm sorry. I'll work as fast as I can."

"Do you want help?" she asked, and I lifted my chin to face her. "I mean, I don't know what I'm doing, but if you need someone to hold something or hand a tool to you, I could probably do that."

The last thing I wanted was to have her right there beside me for the next couple of hours, but then again, was this my chance to show her just what she missed? I had no idea if she was happy with that Blake guy, and I guess I hoped she was, but maybe this was my time to show her what she could have had.

I grinned at her. "Sure, I could use your help, but could I ask a favor?"

She stepped forward, a smile on her face. "Absolutely! Anything!"

That gave me pause as I forced myself to stay on track with my thoughts. "Any chance you could make me some coffee?"

She chuckled and started to walk toward me. "I could use some too. I'll put on a pot." I watched Ali pass me and walk down a short vestibule before she disappeared out a door that led to the front restaurant.

Okay, I could do this. I could be pleasant and chat with Ali and show her the kind of guy I was, and maybe learn how things were going with Blake. Shit! Did I want to know if they were going well? No. The last thing I wanted to hear was about how she was so happy with her choice and that they were doing hunky-dory.

I didn't have a choice, though. Suck it up, buttercup. You got this. If you want to know anything about this woman, you need to listen to what she has to say.

She came back a few moments later, and I was on the ladder, finishing the installation that Alex had been working on. Ali paused as she came back into the room, and I glanced down to see her running her eyes down my body. I slammed my gaze back to the ceiling.

"Coffee is on," she stated a bit huskily and then cleared her throat. "What can I do?"

"Nothing right now, but after I get this up, you can help. Why don't you tell me about the kitchen? How long have you been a chef?" Her job was a safe thing to discuss.

Ali started telling me how she got into cooking as a child, and I listened intently, asking questions every once in a while and laughing at some of things she said. She went to get our coffee, and I came down off the ladder and began to dig through a box to get the next system out. When I opened the box, I jerked back. Taped to the inside of the Styrofoam was a condom.

What. The. Fuck.

I stared at it for a second and heard Ali coming up behind me. Those shits just set me the hell up.

I turned to Ali; she held the coffee mug out to me. "Here you go, just cream as you requested."

It took everything in me to take the coffee mug and put it to my mouth. My entire body screamed for me to take Ali in my arms and put her against my lips, not the damn ceramic mug.

CHAPTER TWENTY-TWO

ALI

"*I* seriously can't believe you didn't tell me he was your brother, or that you were calling him to help!"

"I didn't call him; I called Alice to ask if she knew anyone. I had nothing to do with Harv showing up here."

I glared at her over the table. Holly had come to the restaurant to do a final film blurb about the ending of the romance between Blake and me. It gave me a chance to provide a quick meal as a thank you.

"You knew very well that once you spoke with Alice, that she'd make sure that your brother came here."

"Hey, at least he came. What did you think when you saw him again?"

I peered at the camera crew one table over. They weren't paying us any attention. "I was kind of scattered when I saw him because I wasn't expecting it."

"What did you think of him?"

I stared at her. "I think he was pissed off that he had been kept in the dark too, and that he would have rather been anyplace else."

"Ah." She waved a hand at me. "He was doing the same thing as you. He was surprised to see you and unsure of what to do."

"Well, he sure knew what to do in the end, because he told me that he wished me well and walked out without a look back."

"Did you tell him that you made the wrong choice?"

"No, he didn't give me a chance. When I tried to apologize, he shut me down and left."

"Maybe you will get the chance to tell him when they put the cameras in."

"Oh, I doubt he will come to do it himself. I'm pretty sure he will keep his distance."

Holly grinned at me after a moment. "You never know."

FRIDAY, the restaurant was open—thankfully—and as hard as I tried to keep my head in the game and focused on the cooking, I couldn't. I kept wondering if he would show up tonight once the kitchen was closed, or if he would keep his promise and avoid me.

I was torn on what I wanted. I did want to see Harvey—probably more than I cared to admit—but I also wanted to honor his wishes. He was upset with me; maybe he was glad that I had picked Blake. However, his attitude didn't suggest that. It suggested that he had been hurt. I couldn't blame him; I guess I would have been too. Could we end up being friends?

Before everyone left, I gathered them around and handed out a paper for them to sign. "Hey, guys, I need you all to sign these. The insurance company is requiring us to put cameras up. There will be one in the main kitchen, one near the fridge and freezer, and one at the back door."

Nate, my grill chef, frowned. "Why do they want cameras?"

"After what happened earlier this year with the two

employees stealing, they require us to put them up as our policy renews."

"Why do we need to sign this?" Maryanne, my meat chef, asked.

"Because we need to give permission for them to record sound. We won't do anything with this unless something goes missing. It will all be recorded, and then I can go back and look at it if there is a problem. But I'm not expecting any other problems." I grinned and laughed as if I trusted all of them.

The problem was, I had trusted them, but now as I glanced around, I wasn't sure who I could trust and who I couldn't. God, sometimes it sucked being the boss.

David, my dishwasher, and Wallace, the junior chef, glanced at one another, but it was David that spoke up. "Do we have to sign these?"

"If you want to continue to work here, yes," I stated. Wallace shrugged, but David frowned and then signed the paper.

A few read the form in detail, but most of them passed around a pen and put their John Hancock on the paper without much thought.

I collected the papers and said goodbye to them all. In my office, I set them down and tapped my finger on them. Which one of you is responsible for making my customers sick?

Anton was going to get the waitstaff to sign theirs tomorrow. He questioned me about the insurance, and I'd finally let him in on the real reason for the cameras. He asked if Randolph knew, and I told him that Randolph told me to do what I needed to do to fix the problem. That was good enough for Anton.

So now, the employees were gone, and I sent a text to a phone number that everyone was gone. I was surprised when Harvey and another man arrived, and I hoped that they didn't notice my hands shaking.

I went into my office as soon as I could, hoping to keep myself busy with paperwork that had piled up, but all I could think about was the man in the other room. His voice traveled down the hallway, and I listened like a woman starved for conversation.

He laughed a few times, husky chuckles that oozed right down my spine and into my groin. I rubbed my hands over my face and heard a cellphone ring, and then talking, but I couldn't make out the words until I heard Harvey tell him to go.

I saw Alex rush out the back door and stared at the wall. Oh, my god! I'm alone with Harvey now. Like alone. Like just the two of us. Was this my chance to tell him that I'd made a mistake? My heart started to race as I stood and peeked out the door.

Was he freaking out too? I stared at him for a moment as I stepped out and asked what happened. He looked as nervous as I felt as he explained why Alex had left.

I suggested that I could help him, but didn't expect him to accept it. I assumed he would get all macho and tell me to hide in the office, but he didn't. I happily went to make us some coffee. When I came back, I found him on the ladder, his t-shirt hiked up so that his smooth abdomen was visible. I'd had my hands on that stomach. Oh, my god. I almost licked my lips.

"Coffee is on. What can I do?" Besides begging you to come down that ladder and kiss me again. He stared at me for a minute, and then he looked away and suggested I talk about my job.

Okay, safe subject. Good idea. I started telling Harvey how I started cooking at the age of four, and by ten, I was inventing recipes and never stopped. He seemed genuinely interested and asked questions, chuckling at some of my responses. Each time he did, I had to shift a little to ease the tension building in the base of my spine.

How long was this going to take? Would he be upset if I excused myself and went back to hiding in my office? I wasn't sure I would be able to stick this out.

I went to get the coffee and brought back his mug. When I handed it to him, there was a mysterious glint in his eye as he stared at me. It both excited and scared me, and I stepped away and went to stand on the opposite side of the work station so that it was between us.

"So, I believe your sister said you were in the military."

He nodded and set his mug down. "Yeah, I did twenty, hurt my shoulder right at the end, and retired."

"And now what do you do at the security company? I mean besides install hidden cameras."

He smirked. "Actually, this is not what we normally do."

"What?"

He grinned toward me. "Yeah, the security work that I do is overseas. The company that I work for trains civilians to go into dangerous areas for humanitarian work. Mostly medical situations like clinics and hospitals. Sometimes we train and escort engineers or other people, but mostly medical staff."

"You train them? Like how?"

He went back to work on the cameras. "Mostly educating them on customs, expectations of Americans in the regions they are going, but we also give them some self-defense, weapons, and basic medical training if they need that."

I grinned at him. "You teach people to shoot?" He nodded. "That's kind of cool. I always wanted to learn how to shoot. Alice and Maggie said they would take me some time."

He stared at me. "Alice doesn't know how to shoot."

I laughed. "Yes, she does! She's a competitive shooter."

He stared at me like I had three heads. "Where did you hear that?"

"She told me." I set my mug down and started to walk toward my office. "I'll show you."

I went into my office and collected my cellphone, finding a text from Holly that said, *you're welcome*, with a smiley face. I frowned at the message and then turned around and yelped.

Harvey was standing right behind me, and I'd crashed right into him. "Holy crap! I didn't even hear you come up behind me. Jesus, don't do that; you nearly gave me a heart attack."

"Sorry," he said softly, but the look in his eye didn't seem to go along with that apology. He looked anything but sorry as he stared at me. How easy it would be to lean forward, take one step, and I could be up against his chest again. We continued to stare at one another, and then he finally spoke softly. "You were going to show me something."

I startled out of la-la land and took a step back, returning my attention to my phone. "Yeah, sorry." I tried to bring up the video that Maggie had sent me, but my hands were shaking. Finally, I was able to get my hands to work, and I put the video on the screen and turned it to face him.

He reached for the phone and stared at the video. "Holy shit! Damn, she's good!"

"I haven't seen her in action, but Maggie said she has a ton of trophies. She's been shooting since she was a little girl."

He laughed. "I wonder if Jake knows this. I can't believe that Alice never said anything." He continued watching the video, and I watched him. Holy cow, how had I not noticed just how handsome he really was?

He stepped away and chuckled as he set the phone down on my desk. "That's pretty cool. I'm glad you showed me that. Now I have a way of getting back at Alice." He turned and left the room.

"Getting back at Alice? What do you mean?"

He glanced over his shoulder. "I mean, this whole setup."

I frowned. "What setup?"

He turned so suddenly that I almost crashed into him. His nose flared slightly right before he spoke. "We need to stop doing that."

"Doing what?" I said breathlessly.

His eyes slipped over my face. "Crashing into each other."

"We do seem to have a history of doing that."

"Yes, we do."

I shuffled back half a step. "The first time I saw you, you looked upset. Almost hurt, or maybe it was worried. What was wrong?"

He cocked his head and then rubbed the stubble over his jaw. "I was in a hurry to go help a friend. What made you think I was worried?"

I shrugged a shoulder. "I don't know. I guess it was the look in your eyes. They looked almost haunted, and you seemed very distracted."

He took a half step closer to me. "You saw that?"

I nodded, unable to speak as I had trouble swallowing.

He took another step, and I started to back up, but the counter behind me abruptly halted the process. "How did you see that? People I know can't read me that well."

He was almost against me, and I lifted my chin, staring up into his beautiful green eyes. "I don't know. It's just what I thought when I saw you."

He lifted his hand, a finger tracing down my cheekbone before letting his hand fall back to his side. The feeling went straight to my chest. "Ali, you need to tell me to stop. You need to tell me to back up."

"Why?" My fingers itched with the urge to touch his abdomen. I desperately wanted to run my palms up under his shirt.

"Because if you don't, I can't promise that I won't do something you might regret."

I blinked. "Why would I regret it, and you wouldn't?"

He chuckled ever so slightly. "Because I'm not the one involved with someone."

I straightened my back, bringing my chest closer to his, our mouths only two inches apart. "Try me."

CHAPTER TWENTY-THREE

HARVEY

*S*he did not just say try me. She was so close that all the scents on her clothing mixed with her unique scent spiraled around my head and made it hard to breathe. I should take her face in my hands and bring her lips to mine. I should lift her by the ass and set her on the counter. Ravish her from top to bottom.

My fingers quivered at my sides, and just as I started to reach for her, my cellphone vibrated and brought me back to reality. I stepped away from her quickly, turning my back on her as I pulled my phone out and read the message.

Sorry about taking off on you. Lexi is good—false alarm. Do you want me to come back and help you?

I frowned. Maybe Lexi hadn't been feeling very well, or perhaps it was all part of this master plan to screw with my head. Either way, I wasn't going to let him know that this bothered me. I quickly replied, *No, stay with her. I got this. Glad she is alright. Kiss her for me.*

Will do.

I inhaled sharply and then released it. "That was Alex. Lexi is doing alright."

"How far along is she?"

"About seven months, I think," I replied as I pulled out the last hard-wired camera and set it aside to get the ladder set up.

"And she is married to Alex?"

"Yeah. They got married a few months ago."

"How does she feel about him traveling overseas to dangerous places?" I glanced back at her. If Ali and I were a couple, would she have a problem with that? Stupid question, of course she would, but who cared. It was never going to happen —even if she did dare me to kiss her.

Jesus, she had been so damn close. I should have kissed her again, one more time to see if it still felt the same. Maybe it would be nothing like it had been after that dance. Perhaps I'd made all of that up out of some fancy romantic notion.

I dismissed the thought and answered her questions instead. "He doesn't travel anymore; neither does Trevor. Although both of them will go if they have to, now that they have families, they prefer not to travel. Lexi lost her brother to the war, and when she and Alex were first dating, Alex was held hostage for a while. It didn't bode well for their future until Alex decided Lexi was more important than the job."

"Are all the rest of the guys married? I guess that it would be hard to have someone you love travel to dangerous places all the time."

"Well, Trevor isn't married yet, he's engaged, but he has a son who is about one. Greg and Maggie are together now, but Maggie travels with us."

"Would she travel if she had kids?"

"I don't see them having children," I said, not wanting to share what Greg had told me in confidence. I was now up on the ladder and trying to keep my attention on what I was doing.

"Okay, that makes sense." She paused. "Would you travel if you had kids?"

"Probably. I guess that would depend on the woman I was

with and how much she wanted me to stop what I was doing. My career is pretty important to me."

Ali crossed her arms and leaned back. "Yeah, mine is too." She grew quiet and then slowly started to talk again. "Harvey, let me ask you a hypothetical question."

I chuckled. "Okay, shoot."

"Let's just pretend that we were together, and we wanted to have a child. Would you expect me to quit my job and stay home to raise him or her?"

"No."

She sounded surprised. "You wouldn't?"

I glanced at her. "No. As I said, my career is important, and I would like to think that I would fall in love with a woman who appreciates that and has a love for her own job. I would never try to tell my wife, or girlfriend, or whatever they are what they should do with their career."

"So, you would support them no matter what?"

"Yeah."

She threw her hands in the air. "See! Now that's how a relationship is supposed to be."

I turned back to what I was doing, not wanting to think about her being in a relationship with anyone else. "I take it you haven't seen eye to eye in the past with some men."

"No, I haven't. Pretty much every man I have been even slightly serious with has all but said they would love for me to cook, but I need to cook for them while I'm barefoot and pregnant at home. Some have even tried to get me to quit this job so that I can work more normal hours. They don't realize that these are normal hours for me."

I chuckled; she was cute when she was pissed. I was dying to know if Blake was one of those people, but it wasn't my place to ask.

"What are your normal hours?"

"I'm usually at the restaurant by two, and I'm here until

midnight most nights." She sighed. "I guess that is kind of hard to expect someone else to tolerate if they work a day job."

"It could make a relationship tricky," I replied as I screwed the camera into place.

"Would you be able to deal with it? I mean, if you dated a woman who worked a schedule like me, would you have a problem with it?"

Jesus, I didn't want to think about this. "Probably not, because I have a crazy schedule that she would have to deal with."

She was quiet for a few moments, and then I finished and climbed down the ladder. I set the drill to the side and closed the ladder, laying it on the floor along the wall so it wouldn't tip. When I turned around, she was standing a foot away from me.

Time stood still as we stared each other down. I needed to get this done and get out of here. "Why are you staring at me, Ali?"

"I'm sorry."

"For what?"

"You know what."

"Do I? As far as I know, you could be sorry that you have me here at one-thirty in the morning."

She squinted at me as she pursed her lips. "You know that is not why."

I crossed my arms over my chest and leaned a shoulder against the wall. I had a feeling that until we aired this shit, I wasn't going to get anything else done. I might as well let Ali talk, accept her apology, and then get back to work. "Fine, you don't owe me an apology, Ali. You picked the man that you thought would be the best for you."

"Do you really think that?"

"Think what? I assume that is why you chose Blake. You thought he was the better option. I haven't seen your dances with him, so I have no idea how you two connected with one another. For all I know, you two had a stronger connection than we did."

"No," she said softly and then stepped forward. "We didn't."

I eyed her carefully. What was she saying? What was the point of this whole conversation other than to bring up the pain of not being picked?

"I'm sorry for not choosing you, Harvey. I should have. You were right; I was playing it safe. I was afraid of how you made me feel. Afraid that after it was all over and the excitement wore down, it wouldn't feel the same. That I wouldn't be enough for a man like you."

My lips parted in surprise, and I straightened, my arms falling to my sides slowly as I spoke. "How could you ever think you wouldn't be enough for any man, Ali?"

"I don't know. That's just how I've always felt. Like I couldn't give a man what he wanted because I was also so focused on my own life. I've been called selfish many times because I am devoted to my career."

I shuffled toward her. "Ali, that's not being selfish. That's being true to yourself. You should never give up your dreams for someone else."

"I know," she said as I stopped in front of her.

"Were you really afraid of how I made you feel?"

"Yes."

"How did I make you feel, Ali?" I took in every feature of her face.

"You thrilled me, made my heart pound, and you looked at me like I was your world. Like you would do anything for me, but I'm not sure that I can be that to someone in return."

I touched her cheek; she was very perceptive. At the time that we were dancing, that was pretty much how I had felt. I would have done anything for the woman, and I hadn't even known her.

"What do you feel right now?"

"Like my heart is pounding and I'm afraid that if we kiss, it won't be the same. I'm afraid that it won't feel as perfect as it did, but I want to know. I need to know, Harvey, but I'm afraid." Her hands were on my chest now that she closed the distance. She lifted her lips to mine. "Please."

I speared my hand through her hair and curled my fingers around her neck, holding it right where it was, not allowing her any closer as she stared up at me and begged with her beautiful green eyes.

I would never be able to deny this woman anything. I leaned forward, slowly, slower than I had when we had danced, and our breath mingled. Her hands fisted my shirt, and I wondered if she could feel my heart pounding. Our lips brushed; she quivered in my arms, and I finally sealed my mouth over hers.

I felt things exploding in my head, felt dizzy as I tilted my head more, and opened my lips to mingle my tongue with hers. She whimpered and went up on her tiptoes, pushing her body into mine as she wrapped her arms around my neck and clung to me like I was saving her life from a tidal wave.

I pulled her body flush to mine and ran my palms over her back. From her shoulders to her waist, it felt like I had come home. My hands knew this body, knew how the muscles felt shifting under the material of her clothing. I wanted it all off. I wanted her skin on mine. I wanted to ravish every inch of her body.

A sound of the freezer compressor kicking on reminded me of where we were, and I took her face in mine, slowing the kiss and pulling back to stare down at her.

"Disappointed?" I asked her huskily. She shook her head, and I grinned at her. "Me either, but we need to not do that again. I have work that needs to be finished, and you—" I frowned. I'd never made a move on a taken woman before. I stepped back.

"Well, at least that answered your question. I need to get this done. The minis will only take a few minutes each."

"Alright," she finally replied as I stepped away. "Um, if you'll excuse me, I'm going to finish some paperwork in my office."

"Yeah, sure. I'll let you know when I'm done." She disappeared down the hallway and into her office, and I ran a hand along my jaw. "Well, that was stupid," I said softly to myself before I snagged the box of minis off the floor.

Stupid was an understatement. There was no denying that whatever connection the two of us had when we danced was still there. I don't ever recall kissing a woman that way before and feeling like I should drop to my knees and beg them to let me please them.

I huffed out a sigh and got back to work. With any luck, Ali would stay in her office until I was finished.

CHAPTER TWENTY-FOUR

ALI

I was having an out-of-body experience. That was the only way to explain it. I couldn't feel my body, but my mind was going a hundred miles a minute as I stepped into my office.

Disappointed? Oh, holy hell! How could anyone be disappointed in a kiss like that? The man made me want to climb right up him like he was a telephone pole and hold on as the waves of lust crashed over me. My face tingled, my hands vibrated, and my girlie parts were panting in need.

There was not a man alive that had ever made my body feel like this. I was ready to tear right out of my office and attack him, but I didn't. He still thought that I was with Blake. Maybe after tomorrow, after he watched the show and saw that I had broken it off with him, then he wouldn't hold back.

Man, I did not want him to hold back.

I brushed a hand over my forehead and then sank into my chair. I forced my mind away from Harvey and onto the paperwork sitting on my desk. From time to time, I would hear him moving about and wondered if I should go out and help him.

Yeah, that was a big fat no. I had a feeling that if Harvey

needed my help, he would rather die than ask for it. I yawned and glanced at my watch to see it was after three. I stood and stretched and figured that enough time had passed that I should check on him.

He was whistling softly to himself as he messed with a tablet, and I saw him smile slightly as I approached. "I was just about to get you. I'm sorry it took so long." He lifted his face and looked at me. "You look exhausted."

"I'm okay. I can sleep in. How are things coming?"

"I'm just about done. I was just checking all the camera views." He pushed the tablet toward me, and I looked at all the little squares. Only three had any movement, and those were ones that overlapped with where we were standing.

I turned to see where the camera was. "Where the heck is it?"

He chuckled, stepped around me, and pointed to a screw on the stainless steel. I looked at him. "You're kidding? That screw is the camera?"

"Yep, the lens is painted with a special paint that is see-through for the lens, but people on this side only see the head of the screw."

"That is crazy. Where are the rest of them?"

Harvey walked me around the kitchen, pointing them all out. Then he took me to the fridge and freezer to show me those. There were no cameras inside the units, so we had to hope that whatever was done, was out here in the open somewhere.

"Wow, this is kind of amazing. I'll be able to see everything."

"Yes, but I suggest here at work, you only view the four main cameras. Otherwise, someone else might see all the other views."

I looked up at the ceiling. "Where is the fourth camera?"

"In the employee locker room."

"Oh!" I turned to him. "How will I know if something happens?"

"Well, we can watch it from time to time, but if you think that something might have happened, you let me know, and we can check the video. Just try to give us an approximate time so we can narrow it down. We will start recording tomorrow morning when Mike makes the system live. We will keep the footage until we don't need it anymore."

"Okay, so I guess I have to wait for someone else to get sick. Then I can pull the order and find the times on it."

"Yeah, that would work."

"I hate that someone else is going to need to get sick."

"Yeah, that does suck."

"It's killing my reputation. Ever since I started in this industry, I have had a spotless kitchen, and now I have a bunch of complaints on my name."

"I bet that's hard."

"It's horrible." I sighed. "Okay, what else do you need to do?"

"Just clean up and get someone to pick me up."

"I can take you home."

"Um…" He hesitated, and I put my hand up.

"I can take you home and behave myself. I promise."

"You sure?"

"Absolutely. You load your stuff by the back door, and I'll go make sure everything is off and locked out front, then we can go."

"Alright, if you don't mind."

"Not at all." I hustled out front to turn off the coffee maker and a few lights and then came back to the kitchen to start turning the lights off. Harvey had his tools and two bins by the back door already. I collected my bag from the office and turned off the rest of the lights.

I helped him load his stuff into the back of my SUV and then climbed behind the wheel. The minute he closed the door, I started to freak. Holy crap, we were inside my vehicle together. There was no place to run here.

I gripped the steering wheel tightly and turned the key. "What direction?"

He gave me directions, and we were mostly quiet on the ride to his place. He only lived about fifteen minutes away, and when I pulled into his driveway, I was surprised to see the two-story house. Not sure why I pictured him living in a townhouse or apartment, but I had.

I turned the car off and went to get out, but he put his hand on my arm. "I can get it."

I laughed as I opened my door. "I am quite capable of helping you."

I heard him sigh as I closed the door and rounded the back of my SUV. After I lifted the hatch, I gathered one of the bins, and he took it from my hands.

"What are you doing?"

"Just set them here on the driveway, and I will carry them in."

I stared at him, then glanced at the door. "Is there a reason you don't want me to go into your house?" Did he have someone at home?

"No," he said quickly.

I pulled out the other bin and turned from him. "Then I am helping you carry them inside your house."

"Ali, stop."

I spun around. "Is there something that you don't want me to see inside? Maybe you've been playing me; maybe you are involved with someone."

He laughed. "You're kidding, right?"

"No," I said briskly.

He shook his head and went around me, pausing at the door to unlock it with a keypad that made little beeping noises. He pushed the door open and reached in to turn on a light. As soon as it was on, he set his bin down and told me to put mine next to it as he rushed past me and back to my SUV.

I set the bin down and stepped farther into his house. I was extremely interested in finding out more about the man who fascinated me and made my heart thud erratically.

I heard him groan from behind me. "Thanks, Ali. I got everything now. I appreciate the ride home."

I turned slowly. "You really don't want me in your house, do you?"

"No."

"Why?"

He growled and let his head fall back on his shoulders for a second before he brushed a hand over his beard. The sound that it made gave me goosebumps.

"Ali, can you please just leave? It's late."

I started to walk toward him. "I'll leave after you tell me why you don't want me here."

"It's not that I don't want you here, Ali; it's that I'm having a hard time holding myself back."

Maybe I was naïve, or overly tired, but I asked without thinking, "Holding back from what?"

"From picking you up and carrying you to my room and making you scream my name."

"Oh," I breathed, and his nose flared momentarily.

"So, if you don't mind, I'd like you to leave, please."

I stared at the door. I should go. I should say good night and walk right out that door, but what fun would that be? Not when I was craving the touch of this man.

I turned back to him. "No." Then I walked away from him and toward the stairs.

"Ali, what the hell are you doing?"

"I'm making it easy for you. I'm going up to your room."

"Oh, the hell you are." Suddenly, I was in the air, and he was spinning me and putting me over his shoulder. He turned and was heading back to the door.

"This is your chance, Harvey, our chance. Don't let it go.

Don't you want to know if it will be as incredible as we think it will be?" I was starting to panic. He was going to drop my ass outside on the doorstep, and that would be the end of it.

He stood in the threshold of the door, his hand on the door-knob, and I could feel his heavy breathing under my stomach as his shoulders rose and fell. He could easily plop me on my ass and slam the door in my face, but I trusted that he wouldn't.

"Close the door, Harvey," I said softly as I pushed myself up his back. I felt him shift and then heard the click of the door. "Put me down, Harvey."

His hands came to my waist, and he lifted me slightly, and then my body was sliding down his, precisely as it had during our last dance. Before my feet could hit the floor, I wrapped my legs around his waist, and he slammed his eyes closed and hissed. I felt his arousal nestled between my legs and pressed my hips closer. His hands cupped my buttocks, and he finally looked at me.

"Last chance to leave, Ali."

I tightened the hold around his waist. "I'm not leaving until you have me screaming your name."

I barely got the words out of my mouth before his lips crashed over mine. His arms banded around my body, and I suddenly felt the wall behind me as he pushed against me. Just as I got used to the feel of him, he shifted, and we were moving.

I pulled my mouth away from his and began coating his jaw and neck with kisses, biting under his ear as he started up the steps. I had never been carried up the steps so quickly, and we were barely at the top when he was pulling my hair, removing my mouth from his neck. He directed my mouth back to his, as I saw us pass through a doorway with my partially opened eyes.

A few seconds later, we were falling, and I bounced slightly on his chest as we hit the mattress. He barely paused as he twisted me so that I was under him. Hadn't I already known that he would do that? Hadn't I once thought that he would protect me if I ever fell? What other man would have thought of protecting my body from his weight as we tumbled to the bed? No one that I knew.

Our hands were everywhere, and I arched as he lifted my shirt. It was only then that I thought about how sweaty and dirty I was, but I didn't think that he was going to care.

He pulled back only long enough to remove my shirt, and then he yanked his over his head. His green eyes were dark and intense as he stared down at me, and I shivered. The only light was coming from the hallway, but I didn't need to see. I needed to feel.

I moaned as he slipped down my body, crushing my right breast with his mouth over my bra, before pulling back the cup and latching on to the nipple again. I held him there, needing him as I squeezed my legs around his waist.

He let that one go, rolling us to the center of the bed on our sides so that he could unlatch the back. He started to shift me to my back again, but I pushed him to his instead, and rolled on top of him, pressing my groin down against his throbbing length.

He lifted his head, tasting one breast then the other, burying his face between them as he licked his way around. He picked me up off his hips, tossing me to the side and making me giggle. A moment later, I saw the smile as his mouth returned to mine, and his hands pulled at the waistband of my leggings.

I wiggled out of them, loving the feel of his rough cargo pants against my sensitive flesh. He pulled me to the edge of the bed as he went to his knees between my legs. He was masterful, making me climb swiftly to the point of explosion, and then he paused. "Don't forget to scream it, baby."

My hands went to the back of his head and pulled him forward again; a few seconds later, I did what he asked. I screamed his name as I wriggled over the mattress. My only thought was that he wouldn't kick me out now that I had.

CHAPTER TWENTY-FIVE

HARVEY

*I*t was rough sitting next to her in the car, but when we arrived at my house and she wanted to help me bring things in, well, I wasn't sure I wanted that. Okay, so I wanted it—and a whole lot more, but I didn't think it was wise.

She walked away with a bin in her hands, and I stared at the subtle swish of her hips. This woman was trouble; I could feel it —and damn—did I want her kind of trouble.

I was trying to do the right thing here, trying to be a gentleman, but she just had to push. Her green eyes were bright as she stared at me and told me she wasn't leaving. I wanted to carry her to the door, set her down safely outside, and then step back and bolt every lock on my door, but I didn't.

I caved.

I lost myself in that first kiss. I was consumed by the feel of her body against mine. The fire that raged inside of me wasn't going out anytime soon. I carried her up the stairs, needing something from her—needing everything from her.

I stripped her of her clothing, barely taking the time to remove my shirt before I was lapping at her sensitive flesh. Her hands cupped the back of my head, urging me on, her legs squeezing the sides of my face at times, and then as she broke apart, the awe-inspiring sound of her screaming my name.

"Harvey! Oh, god, Harvey, please!"

She wriggled against me, and I could tell she was torn between wanting more and needing distance to calm herself. I kissed the inside of her thigh, licked down to her knee, nipped at the skin there, and she giggled. Her giggle went straight to my chest, and I closed my eyes and just absorbed it. I memorized the sound of it, and then the guilt crashed down on me, and I sighed as I rested my forehead on her leg.

I should not have done this. Ali wasn't mine. Yes, she had wanted it too, had pushed for this, but was she the kind of woman that I wanted if she'd cheat on another guy? No, absolutely not.

My god, I had been part of it. I had given in to my desire for her, as hard as my cock throbbed, as much as I wanted to be balls deep in her, I couldn't do it. This was wrong, so damn wrong.

I lifted my head, took one last look at her beautiful body, and then I was on my feet, and I was grabbing my shirt. I tossed her shirt to the bed and pulled mine on as a look of shock crossed her features.

"What are you doing?" Her voice was husky, and I cringed. No, I was not going to back down on this. I didn't condone cheating. I had already broken that vow with her temptation, but I would not go any further.

"You need to go, Ali."

"Harvey, what are you talking about? We are not done."

"Yes, we are." I walked out of the room without looking back. I did everything that I could to keep my mind and body healthy. What I had just done was not good for my heart or my soul. I had allowed temptation to cloud my judgment. Damn it! I went straight to the stairs and down to the first floor. There I popped into the powder room off the living room and washed my face and hands and stared at myself in the mirror. What an ass you are!

As I was coming out of the bathroom, I heard the floor upstairs creaking. I went into the kitchen and pulled a beer out of the fridge, jerking the cap off and then guzzling over half of it the first time I tipped it up.

I set the bottle down hard on the counter and placed both palms on either side of it, hanging my head. I was hyper-vigilant on the sounds upstairs, and when I heard her on the stairs, I braced myself. She was going to be pissed, but whatever. She could be angry with me all she wanted. I wasn't the one that had just cheated on someone.

I stood in the archway between the kitchen and living room and braced one arm on the wall as she reached the first floor. She turned to look at me, but what I saw there almost took me to my knees. It wasn't anger; it was sadness and confusion and hurt. We stayed where we were, neither of us moving or speaking.

A tear eased from her eye and started to blaze a path down her cheek, and I almost stepped forward. I had hurt her. That wasn't my intention. God, I was such an asshole. Before I could do or say anything, she jerked her head to the side, swiped at the wetness, and then walked to the door. She paused at the door as if waiting for me to do or say something, but I remained where I was. I could not be with someone who would cheat on another person, no matter how good or bad a relationship was.

She started to glance back, but stopped herself, and instead let her gaze fall to the bins. I saw her lips purse, saw her nod just the slightest bit, and then she jerked the door open and walked out. She didn't even close the door, just walked through it and kept going.

I didn't move from my spot until I heard her engine turn over, and headlights flashed into the room, making a wavey pattern through the entryway as she pulled out of the driveway and drove away. I listened to the sound of her engine fade, and only when I could hear nothing but the night did I move toward the door.

I closed it and turned the lights off, going up the stairs to my room. I stared at the messy bed and turned away from it, going into the bathroom and straight to the shower. I tried not to think about her, tried not to recall her scent or her taste, or the sound of her voice as she said my name. I didn't want to relive every minute of her time in my house, but I did. Over and over again—and I came twice in the process.

When I finished my shower, I returned to my bedroom, grabbed my pillow, and turned the lights out. I went into the guest room two doors down and curled up on the bed.

I had wanted that woman beyond reason. Unfortunately, my reasoning had come back to me, and at the moment, I wasn't sure if I was happy or sad about that. I hated that I had hurt her, but what else was I supposed to do. If she could cheat on Blake, she could cheat on me, and that was not okay. I closed my eyes, shut down my mind, and drifted off to sleep.

* * *

I WOKE to the pounding on the front door and glanced at my watch. Shit, it was ten. I rolled off the bed and stretched my back. There was a reason this bed was in here and not in my bedroom. It sucked! I glanced around as I went, unsure where my cellphone was, and as I got to the first floor, I saw it on the side table.

Another round of pounding filled the air. "Hold your damn horses, I'm coming!" I partially shouted and growled at the same time as I glanced at the screen on my phone. There were a bunch of missed calls and texts, but I ignored them to pull open the door. "What?"

Alex stood on the other side. "You're alive. You alone?"

"Yes, I'm alone. Did you forget that I was working on the cameras until after three in the morning?"

"No, I didn't forget, but you never miss a text or call. I was just going to let you know that I was dropping your truck off, but you didn't answer."

"So you came over here to pound on my door? What if I wasn't home?"

Alex cocked his head and started to smile. "Where else would you be?"

I glared at him and then walked away from the door. I needed coffee, and I wasn't in the mood to play games. Yes, I had fallen asleep relatively fast, but I'd woken up about five or six times and hadn't gotten all that much sleep.

"How is Lexi?"

"She's fine," he stated. "How did it go last night?"

I stared at him for a moment and then went back to pouring the water into the coffee maker. "Before I answer that, I want to know if Lexi really had an issue last night, or if that was a setup to get Ali and I together?"

"Did it work?"

"You're an ass. All of you are assholes." I grunted. "The system is up and running. It just needs Mike to make it live."

"It's already live."

"Is it?"

"Yeah, Mike did it first thing this morning."

"Does it look alright?"

He shrugged. "I have no clue. I guess we will see how it does today when her employees are there. You might need to go in and adjust a camera or two."

"Not me. Get someone else to do it."

"Um..." He paused, and I stepped away and opened the fridge to pull out the makings of my green shake. "I thought that things were okay with you two. Did something happen last night?"

I wanted to burst out laughing. "No."

"No?"

I grabbed the soy milk and put it on the counter next to my greens. "No, I would just prefer for someone else to do it."

"Harv, did something happen last night?"

"I told you no."

"Alright, well, I guess if you don't want to see her again, I can do it."

The idea of anyone else being around her in the middle of the night irked me something fierce, but Ali wasn't my problem —and she sure as hell wasn't mine to worry about.

"Where is the tablet?"

"In the top bin near the door," I told him, and he went to get it while I put all my ingredients into my blender. I added protein powder to it and was getting ready to hit the button when Alex came back into the kitchen.

"Looks like the cameras are working." He held the tablet out toward me, and I zeroed in on Ali moving around the kitchen.

She glanced up at one of the cameras, and her lips were moving. "What is she saying?"

"Don't know," Alex said and pushed a button on the screen to see if he could pick up the microphone. The small ones didn't have sound, but the main ones did.

We could just make out what she was saying, and Alex turned it up. "I guess it doesn't matter; you did it for your own reasons. I might never know what they were or why you demanded that I leave, but I have to respect your wishes."

"I assume she is talking about you?" Alex said in question, and I hushed him as she continued.

"I wondered for a long time this morning if maybe I had been the only one to feel it, and that's why you kicked me out."

"You kicked her out?" Alex asked quickly.

"Shut up!" I hissed at him as I took the tablet from his hands and walked away. She looked like she hadn't slept all night, either. That was no doubt my fault.

She sighed. "I thought you had, but I guess I was fooling myself." She shook her head. "See, that's part of my problem; I think that when I feel something, someone else might too. That's why I decided to do this stupid dancing show anyway. I thought maybe without words, with just movement, I might find someone who was perfect for me."

She frowned, and I sank onto my sofa. I felt Alex step behind the couch and knew he was watching. I didn't care. I only cared what she had to say.

She glanced up, her green eyes wary. "I sure thought I did. I mean, I know I told you that I was sorry and that I had chosen wrong, but what Blake and I—"

I turned off the speaker before I could hear what she had to say. I didn't want to know what Ali and Blake had together. It didn't matter. Her words didn't matter. I tossed the tablet to the couch cushion and started toward the stairs.

Alex grabbed my arm and pulled me to a stop. "What the hell is wrong with you?"

"Nothing, I need a shower. I don't have time to listen to her boohoo about how she picked Blake and doesn't know what to do now."

"What happened with you two last night?" he asked.

"Nothing."

Alex laughed. "That sure didn't sound like nothing. Did you sleep with her when she brought you home?"

"No!"

"Did you kick her out before you could sleep with her?"

I rubbed my hands up and down over my face and then sighed. "She came in, she pushed the limit. I didn't give her anything she didn't ask for."

Alex frowned and shoved my shoulder. "Ask for? What the hell did you do, Harv? Did you hurt her?"

"Whoa, I would never physically hurt a woman."

"Then what the fuck did you do, man?"

I turned and plopped my ass on the second step. "Ali pushed me last night, and I told her that she needed to leave, or I was going to have her screaming my name. She refused to leave, so I took her upstairs and made her scream my name. We didn't have sex, though. That's when I told her to leave."

"Why would you do that?"

"Because she's still with Blake!" I jumped to my feet. "I don't do cheats, Miller. I forgot about it just long enough to lose my head, but then I remembered before it was too late. I am not that kind of guy. I will not be *that* guy."

CHAPTER TWENTY-SIX

ALI

*W*hat was going on? Why did he want me to leave? Was he seriously going to walk out of here? I stared at the empty doorframe, heard a board creak on the wooden steps, and realized he honest to god was.

What in the hell just happened? Didn't he want this? Had I been mistaken?

Holy crap! I must have been! What a fool he must think I am to throw myself at him as I did. I gathered the rest of my clothes and quickly dressed. Where were my car keys? I looked around and then put my hands to my face. I had left them and my purse in the car. Talk about sidetracked!

He wanted me to leave, then fine, I would leave. I lifted my chin and went down the stairs. At the bottom, I stared at him from across the room. My body still screamed for him, my heart wanted to wrap itself around him, but it was so damn obvious that he didn't want that. His features were hard, stormy almost, and they were like a knife to the heart.

I had been so wrong about this man. How could I have thought that we would be good together? How could I possibly have thought that dancing with a stranger would have found me someone to love. The blade in my heart twisted. As I continued to stare at him, there were so many emotions in his eyes, but his face was blank. I didn't understand any of this. I realized that I was about to walk away from a man that I could have loved with my entire soul, and my heart ached. For that man, I might have done anything.

A tear crept out and slipped slowly down my cheek. Did he see it, did he care? I turned away and wiped it as I went to the door. I opened the door, but I didn't bother to close it. I was too broken at the moment to care. It was drizzling outside as I rushed to my car and jumped inside.

I turned the key with shaking hands, my eyes as blurry as the windshield before I turned on the wipers, and then I pulled out of his driveway and drove away. I didn't stop driving until I arrived at my house, and then I grabbed my purse, went in through the garage door, and promptly slipped to the floor and sobbed.

After a few moments of self-pity, I picked myself up and went to take a shower. I forced myself not to think about Harvey—almost succeeded until I climbed under the sheets.

Then the entire night began to play over and over again, and it was just as I was falling asleep that I realized what had happened. He had mentioned Blake and me earlier in the night, and I hadn't corrected him. Had he pushed me away because his conscience had gotten the better of him? Had he thought that I was still with Blake?

No wonder there was malice and disgust in his eyes as I left his place. He thought I was cheating on Blake. Holy crap. I needed to figure out a way to fix this. It was only after I thought I had it figured out that I finally drifted off to sleep.

The next day, I was up earlier than I wanted and headed straight into the restaurant. Today I needed to oversee the inventory and approve the menu for the next week. Once a month, we made significant purchases of all the dry ingredients that we would need for the coming weeks. Then every week, we brought in perishables, and meat arrived almost daily, along with more in-season vegetables.

When I stepped into the kitchen, I paused and glanced at the camera on the ceiling pointed at me. It was odd knowing that everything we did would be recorded now, but that was for the safety of our patrons. I winced as I walked under it and to my office.

Before I got busy with paperwork, I went into the kitchen and started preparing a brunch meal for my employees. They would be here soon, and those who volunteered to come in early today always received a free meal before we got to work.

I had pulled out my favorite knife and was starting to dice vegetables when I glanced up and noted the screw. An idea came to me of how I might be able to reach Harvey. I had no clue if there was any audio, but maybe there was. I also had no idea who would watch this, or if it was even on yet, but it was the least I could do. I would need to be careful in what I would say, though. I didn't think he'd want his friends to know what happened between us.

Would he see it? I had no clue, but maybe if he wasn't watching and someone else was, they would tell him. If there were no audio, then people would think I liked to randomly talk to myself—which wasn't too far off.

I glanced at the screw again. "Alright, so maybe you are watching, and you can hear me, if not whoever is watching might think I'm crazy, but this is the only way I know how to talk to you right now."

I took a deep breath. "I don't know why you did what you did last night. Maybe I pushed you too hard, or maybe you had a weak moment and gave in. Who knows. I guess it doesn't particularly matter; you did it for your own reasons. I might never know what they were or why you demanded that I leave, but I have to respect your wishes."

I paused for a second. "I wondered for a long time this morning if maybe I had been the only one to feel it, and that's why you kicked me out." I sighed after a moment. "I thought you had, but I guess I was fooling myself. See, that's part of my problem. I think that when I feel something, someone else might too. That's why I decided to do this stupid dancing show anyway. I thought maybe without words, with just movement, I might find someone who was perfect for me."

I thought over what I wanted to say next. "I sure thought I did. I mean, I know I told you that I was sorry and that I had chosen wrong, but what Blake and I had on the dance floor was exactly what you had said, it was safe. It was also very wrong. He isn't the one that I want. He never really was. I want sexy and exhilarating, and a man who can make my toes curl with a kiss and someone who can make me scream their name."

I pulled my bottom lip under my teeth as I felt my cheeks warm; that is exactly what he had done to me. I kept my eyes down on my task as I continued. "I wanted a man who wouldn't try to make me change but would help me find ways to adapt my life into theirs. Someone who appreciated how hard I worked for my career and who saw eye to eye with me."

I set the knife down and stared at the camera lens. "I found that. I found it in you, Harvey. I should never have picked Blake, but what you don't know is that I broke it off with him several days ago, and today when the show airs, the entire world will know that I chose wrong. I should have gone with my heart and not my head. I should have chosen you, Harvey. I should have told you that I wanted the next dance with you, and the one after that, and the one after that, and the one that lasts forever."

I hesitated for a few seconds. "I hope you see this. I hope that whoever sees this will put your ass in a chair and make you watch it. I want what we started on that dance floor. I want what we shared last night so briefly. I want you."

The back door opened, and I quickly glanced at the camera

and whispered, "There is only one more thing for me to say. I want you to come to me, and I want you to ask me for the next dance, Harvey. Can you do that? Will you do that?"

I shifted away as Malick called out my name and said good morning.

"Hey, Malick, how are you this morning?"

He pointed at the ceiling. "Those went up pretty fast."

I chuckled. "Yeah, they went up last night."

"How late were you here?" he asked as he came around the counter. "What are we making this morning?"

"Three, and I thought I would do a quiche. Do we have any leftover ham? We could add some of that."

"Yes, we do, on it, Chef!" he said. With that, I forgot about Harvey, the cameras tucked into every nook and cranny, dancing and the show, and focused on what mattered right now: cooking breakfast and taking care of my kitchen.

* * *

DINNER WAS in full swing when David popped his head into the kitchen. "Ali, you're on television!"

I glanced at the clock, well, I guess it was on. Too bad I wasn't going to be able to see it. I'd have to wait until I got home and watch the recording that I had set up earlier this week.

"Um, David, how do you know that I'm on television? Did you get one back in the scrub room?"

"Nah, I just got a text from my girlfriend. She said she's watching it."

"Alright, well, put your phone away and get back to work. You can see the rerun later."

"You going to tell us which guy you picked?" Melinda asked. Because of our contracts, Blake and I had kept our relationship quiet from all our friends, except Charlie. She was the only one that knew. Everyone I worked with just knew that I was dating someone, and I would announce it when I could.

I pondered that question for a moment. "Let's just say that I followed my head and not my heart, and I probably shouldn't trust my head when it comes to romance."

Melinda chuckled. "I saw the previews of it; was it the short brown-haired guy, the dark-haired guy, or the blonde that you did choose?"

I sighed. "I chose Blake, the blonde."

"Oh, he was an attractive guy," Melinda stated, and Wallace frowned at her.

"Hey, Wallace, you do know that we are allowed to look at other men, just like you are allowed to look at other women, right? You just can't touch," I said, and a few people laughed. Sadly, the comment out of my own mouth reminded me of last night and what Harvey must have thought of me.

"See?" Melinda glanced at her boyfriend, who rolled his eyes.

"Yeah, right, like that will happen. You just knocked me upside the head the other day for checking a woman out."

"You were drooling over her, Wallace. There is a difference between checking someone out and saying they are attractive and undressing someone with your eyes."

More laughter skittered around the room. "Okay, guys, can we get back to our jobs and leave the romance in the alley for a little while longer? We are really close to getting behind, and we can't afford that right now, not with everything else going on."

"Yes, Chef." A few people commented, and then the conversation was back to what was up, what was new, who needed what, why were the capers not where they were supposed to be, and so on.

Ricardo took my station a few times, as I hit the restaurant floor, speaking to patrons, checking things, and dealing with an inventory issue. By the end of the night, I was whipped, and I didn't even bother to update reports.

After my lack of sleep last night, I needed to hit the sack early, and I could come in tomorrow morning and catch up. I barely made it back to my place before I couldn't keep my eyes open, but once I was inside and climbing into bed, my gaze drifted over my television, and I remembered the show.

Yes, I had seen the dances, but I hadn't seen during practices or before and after the dances. I grabbed the remote, fluffed up my pillow, and hit play. There would be no way to sleep knowing it was there on my recorder, not now. Not until I saw every moment I could of Harvey.

CHAPTER TWENTY-SEVEN

HARVEY

I had turned the show on, then turned it off, then turned it back on again. I walked out of the room, returned, went to get a beer, sat down, stood back up, and then left my beer on the table, grabbed my keys and my phone, and walked out the door.

I couldn't watch it. Part of me wanted to. The sick part of me wanted to replay the whole thing. Maybe I could evaluate everything I did and see where I screwed up? Perhaps I could understand why she chose the way she did. I could see what she saw in Blake, see the connection the two of them had.

And then there was the other part of me that said who the fuck cared. It wasn't my problem. Ali wasn't someone that I wanted in my life if she could cheat on a man she had only been with for a few weeks.

I drove down to the local tavern and grabbed a stool at the end of the crowded bar. I was about halfway through my beer when a woman tapped me on the shoulder. I turned to see her looking excited but nervous. "Are you him?"

"Am I him?" I asked as I laughed. "Who do you think I am?"

She pointed to the television behind me in the corner, where Ali and I were about to dance the second dance. Holy shit!

"No," I muttered as I spun back around, and she put her hand on my arm.

"It is you."

I closed my eyes to keep myself calm and not lash out. "Yeah, so it's me."

Why I hadn't heard it before, I don't know, but now—even over the din of the tavern—I could hear Tarin talking and myself answering right before I went on.

I couldn't help myself, I shifted in my seat and stared up at the television. The music started, and I watched it, slightly breathlessly, as our dance began. I felt like I was having an out-of-body experience as I watched our bodies move and remembered the feel of her body, the heat of the light, the volume of the music.

I was more mesmerized now as I watched Ali than I had been that night. I had kissed that woman, held her in my arms. I'd had her body under mine—naked. I had tasted her sweetness, heard her scream from pleasure—my name on her lips as she shattered. I could have had her completely, but I had walked away. Was that smart or stupid?

People clapped for me, and all around me people wanted to touch me. Why I had no clue, but they did. I was in awe of the kiss on the screen, and I couldn't believe they kept the part where I stood there staring after her. What a lovestruck fool I looked like.

My after-dance interview just added flame to the fire, and I hoped that the guys that I worked with were not watching this. Damn, I could imagine what they would all say.

Then I watched Ali after she came off the floor. She looked just as shocked as I had by our dance—by our kiss. I should have felt vindicated, but I didn't because I knew that I lost.

I wanted to turn away, not watch anymore, but I couldn't

help myself. I had to see how Ali and Blake danced. I needed to know what safe looked like.

So I had them refill my beer and add a shot to it. Then I sat there and watched Ali and Blake dance. They were striking as a couple, so different, but still beautiful to watch. They did look good together, not as good as we did—at least in my opinion— but who cared what I thought.

When they were done, several people were watching me, and the lady who had gathered my attention in the first place stepped closer, lowering her voice. "She didn't pick you, did she?"

"What makes you say that?"

"Because you're here, and not with her. I have a feeling that if she had picked you, the two of you would have weathered any storm to make it work."

I stared at her. "What makes you think that?"

She shrugged. "I don't know. It's just the way you two look at one another. Like the other person is everything to you—or could be. Like you would move heaven and earth to be there for them. That other guy, yeah, maybe he could make her happy, but not forever."

I laughed. "Yeah, well, you're right. Ali didn't pick me. I came here to get away from this so that I didn't have to watch it."

"Well, I think it's better that you watch it, and afterward, I'm sure you can have your pick of women here in the bar." She waved a hand around, and I scanned the area, noting several women who were watching me.

I turned back around as they returned from commercial and did a few interviews with us. Again, I didn't want to watch, but I got pulled in by the excitement of the crowd. The woman beside me, who introduced herself as Carol, grabbed the stool next to me, and we chatted during commercials. She was nice, but not my type, and I was glad that she wasn't trying to flirt with me.

She seemed to be more interested in friendship, and I was okay with that.

When it came time for Ali to meet up with her choice, I tensed. Damn, I did not want to watch this, but I was not able to look away. As I received the card that thanked me but said sorry, there was a ton of boos in the group from everyone around me, and I found myself laughing.

I watched her meeting Blake and a few minutes of chat before they walked off into the park. Well, that was it. She had made her choice. I turned back to the bar, and Carol punched my arm. "You have to watch the update. Maybe they broke up."

"No, they didn't."

"Do you know that for sure?"

I shrugged, and when the update came on, I turned to watch it. What I heard caused my jaw to drop. Ali was speaking with Tarin at the restaurant, dressed in her chef's coat. "Blake and I had a great friendship right from the start, and we really enjoyed our time, but we realized that we were much better as friends than we were anything else." Ali laughed softly. "My best friend told me I should have gone with sexy and not safe. I think I should have listened to her."

People were staring at me, and I could do nothing but stare at the screen. Ali and Blake weren't together anymore? What? Why didn't she tell me? Why didn't she say something?

"You okay?" Carol asked, and I jerked back to reality.

"Yeah, yeah, I'm good. Look, it was great talking to you, Carol, but I gotta go."

She smiled. "I bet I know where you are going."

I laughed. "Well, that makes one of us." I kissed her cheek, thankful that she had tapped me on the shoulder and made me watch it. "Maybe we will see each other again."

"I hope so, Harvey. Good luck!" she called out as I made a beeline out of the tavern and to my truck.

Now to figure out how to deal with this. I returned to my

house and located the laptop that I had tossed aside. After plugging it in, I turned the program on and watched her move through the kitchen as she worked.

I tried to come up with a plan of how to apologize for being such an ass. What could I do to fix what I'd done? No wonder she looked heartbroken when she left here, but why didn't she tell me? Why didn't she just say she wasn't with Blake anymore? It would have been so easy, and everything would have been different.

I tried not to think about what would have happened if she had told me, because I didn't need my hormones jacked any higher than they were already.

Instead, I watched her work through the night and leave. I had no clue where she lived, so it wasn't like I could find her right now. Suddenly, I remembered that earlier today, she had been talking to me. I found the recorded files on our server and started listening to them again from the moment she came into work.

I found the place that I had turned off the sound and listened again. "I sure thought I did. I mean, I know I told you that I was sorry and that I had chosen wrong, but what Blake and I had on the dance floor was exactly what you had said; it was safe. It was also very wrong. He isn't the one that I want. He never really was. I want sexy and exhilarating, a man who made my toes curl with a kiss, and someone who could make me scream their name."

Shit!

"I wanted a man who wouldn't try to make me change but would help me find ways to adapt my life into theirs. Someone who appreciated how hard I worked for my career, and who saw eye to eye with me."

What was she saying here? She stared into the lens and continued. "I found that. I found it in you, Harvey. I should never have picked Blake, but what you don't know is that I broke it off with him several days ago, and today when the show airs, the entire world will know that I chose wrong. I should have gone with my heart and not my head. I should have chosen you, Harvey. I should have told you that I wanted the next dance with you, and the one after that, and the one after that, and the one that lasts forever." She paused. "I hope you see this. I hope that whoever sees this will put your ass in a chair and make you watch it. I want what we started on that dance floor. I want what we shared last night so briefly. I want you."

I heard a door open, and her eyes jumped to the back of the room and then came back. I had to adjust the volume to hear what she said next. "There is only one more thing for me to say. I want you to come to me, and I want you to ask me for the next dance, Harvey. Can you do that? Will you do that?"

I sat back and smiled as she started talking to a guy named Malick about breakfast. An idea began to form in my mind, and I smiled for the first time since yesterday.

I picked up the phone and called Mike. "Hey, I need your help with something."

"Yeah, I'm kind of busy right now."

"Mike, I'm telling you that I need your help. You all got me into this mess, and now you all need to help me get out."

He was quiet for two seconds. "You're right; what do you need?"

CHAPTER TWENTY-EIGHT

ALI

$\mathcal{I}$t had been three days since the show aired, and I hadn't heard from Harvey. Maybe he hadn't seen it? Maybe the video hadn't been live when I'd done my little impromptu speech on Saturday night. I fretted over it when I wasn't feeling the pins and needles under my backside to see when the next person would get sick.

When the kitchen wasn't open for business, I was personally going through each station and sterilizing it over and over again. I knew that by now, I had cleaned every inch of the room —twice. I had even gotten up on the ladder and sanitized the fans, the lights, and the ceiling panels.

I documented every single thing I did and knew that video was recording my every move. If only I didn't have to wait for someone else to get sick to figure out what was going on.

The last couple of days, business had been busier than usual, and quite a few people had asked to speak to me. Not about the food, but about my experience on the show. Who knew doing that show would help business? Several of the women I spoke with made sure to let me know that they would have chosen Harvey over Blake in a minute. Didn't they know I knew that already? Didn't I say in the show that I had chosen wrong? I was pretty sure that I had. Two women even asked me if I knew how to get in touch with Harvey. I smiled politely, told them no, and wished them a good meal.

I was frustrated with the whole situation. I had assumed that word would have gotten to Harvey, even if it was by Alice or Maggie, that I wasn't with Blake anymore, but so far nothing. I hadn't even heard from Holly in the last couple of days. I was starting to conclude that he just wasn't interested.

Which made no flipping sense! After what happened with us Friday night, it was so evident that he felt something for me. Was he denying it? Did he feel guilty for the way he had treated me after? Was he just an inconsiderate ass?

I winced. I didn't want to think of Harvey that way. I didn't believe that he was inconsiderate, not if he was Holly's brother. Yes, siblings could be very different, but I didn't think they would be total opposites.

I stared at my kitchen, my arms tired from scrubbing, my hair hanging around my face in frizzy wisps. I don't think my kitchen had ever been so clean. The back door opened, and Ricardo came in, shaking the rain off his jacket.

"Whoa, you might want to open the back door and get some fresh air in here. That stuff is pungent."

"Really?" I sniffed. "I guess I've been breathing it so long I don't even notice anymore. Crack the back door and reposition that back fan to blow out."

"Sure. Why are you cleaning again?"

"Because I'll be damned if someone else is going to get sick from something in my kitchen."

He was positioning the fan and glanced back. "You ever think that it might not be the kitchen, but the food?"

"Of course, I have thought of that, but do you hear of any other patrons getting sick at other restaurants? It's not like any of our suppliers only supply us."

He nodded. "Didn't the Health Department say they were going to close us for two weeks if anyone else got sick?"

"Yes, and I'm doing everything I can to make sure that doesn't happen. We need to stay on top of everyone. I want people to scrub their hands like they are about to perform surgery and clean uniforms and aprons every single day. I'm not taking any chances, Ricardo. I can't afford to."

"You're doing all that you can, Ali. What does Randolph say?"

"He's worried, but he thinks I can handle it. Says that I should keep doing what I'm doing."

"What is he going to do if they close us down for two weeks?"

I shrugged and sighed. "I have no clue, but I have a feeling I'd be looking for a new job."

Ricardo squeezed my shoulder. "That won't happen. I think after the scrubbing you gave this kitchen, the patrons could eat off any surface they wanted to without any issues."

We both laughed, and then a few other people started to arrive. I went back to the employee restroom and washed my face, brushed my hair, and changed out of my t-shirt into a camisole that I wore under my chef's coat. Twenty minutes later, I was in the center of the kitchen and preparing for another busy night.

Around eight-thirty, amid our busiest time, there was banging at our back door, and before David could answer it, Anton rushed into the kitchen with a paramedic and a policeman.

"What's going on?" I asked him as I sprinkled seasoning over the dish in front of me.

David's voice raised as he yelled from the back door, "Chef!"

I turned to see several cops coming down the hallway toward us. "What the hell is going on?"

One of the police officers was on the phone and said, "Which one?" He paused and then nodded. "Yeah, I got him."

Two police officers walked over to Ricardo, who started sputtering. "What are you doing? I haven't done anything wrong."

"What the hell is going on!" I shouted, trying to get someone to tell me something.

The paramedic rushed to my side. "I need to know what he was cooking and who got it?"

"What?" I grabbed the cop's arm as he started to pulled Ricardo away. "Wait! Will someone just tell me what the hell is going on, please?"

The cop looked pointedly at my hand and then at me; I let him go but didn't back down, and he sighed. "This man was seen on camera putting something into the food."

"Excuse me?" I asked, and then it dawned on me, and I automatically glanced at the camera at his station. "Who called you?"

"We got a call from your security company, ma'am."

The paramedic stepped forward. "You can help yourself out a lot here if you tell me what meal you poisoned."

"Wait! You think Ricardo did this? No! He's my sous chef! He would never do this!"

I stared at him, but Ricardo refused to meet my eyes. The cop pulled him around toward the paramedic as the officer spoke. "You realize that if he dies, you will be charged with homicide."

"He won't die! I only gave him enough to make him sick."

I gasped. "Ricardo! Why would you do that?"

"Why do you think? I was never going to get the head chef position with you here. I need you out of the way. I was hoping Randolph would fire you for negligence."

I stepped forward and smacked him across the face. A moment later, one of the police officers was pulling me back from him. "You deserve to be in jail! How could you do that to someone? How could you do that to me? After everything that I have done for you! You tried to ruin my reputation! You screwed around with all of your co-worker's lives and with our customers! They trusted us to feed them healthy food, and you poisoned them!"

"What meal was it, Ricardo?" the paramedic asked again. "We know it was a chicken meal."

Ricardo clamped his mouth shut, but one of the waitresses stepped forward. "I served four chicken meals about ten minutes ago."

"How many other chicken meals have gone out in the last fifteen minutes?" Anton asked as he glanced over the rest of the waitstaff who had gathered right inside the kitchen door.

"I had two, but I just put them down on the table."

"I had one; the rest of mine have been beef and seafood," another waitress stated.

I turned to Malick. "How many chicken meals have you plated in the last fifteen minutes?"

He seemed to think for a moment. "Only seven."

The paramedic nodded and turned toward the waitstaff. "Please take me to the tables where they were served."

While he rushed out into the dining room, Anton hot on his heels, Ricardo was ushered out of the kitchen in handcuffs. A police officer asked where the employees stored their things, and I showed him, pointing out Ricardo's items. He gathered all of his things, stating that they were going to keep them until they got a search warrant to go through them.

"How did he do it?"

"The guy on the phone said that he came back here and put a glove on. He had watched enough to know they don't normally wear gloves, and not in the locker room. Then the guy was in his stuff briefly before he hurriedly walked out of here and to his station. He stuck his finger into the food, then removed the glove." He walked over to a trash can and lifted a few things before retrieving a plastic baggie with a glove inside from the trash. "And put it into a baggie, tossed it here, and then went to wash his hands."

The last few minutes ran through my mind. I remembered him walking away and coming back, then I glanced up as I put a seafood platter next to a chicken plate and saw him washing his hands.

"I know what plate it was. The other diner at his table had a seafood plate." Malick nodded and rushed out of the kitchen into the dining room.

"So Ricardo was getting the E. coli on his finger and then putting it into the food?" I rubbed my temple. "I can't believe he would do that to me. Of everyone in my kitchen, it was him that I trusted the most."

"I'm sorry about that. I need to get a little more information from you if you don't mind."

"Yeah, let me get the kitchen shifted around." I turned back to the kitchen, but as I looked around, the staff was already back to work. All of them quiet, several frowning as if they couldn't believe what had happened. Well, stand in line. "You guys know what to do."

I turned and walked into my office. We had been short before, and we were on the decline with meals coming in at this time of night, so I knew that they could handle it.

The officer and I sat in my office, and I explained everything that had happened while giving him copies of all the reports from the Health Department and explaining about the cameras.

"Those cameras were a good idea, and the guy on the other end was observing. As soon as he saw something out of the ordinary, he called us."

"Do you know who called?"

He glanced at his notes. "Mike Johnson, Safety Zone Security."

I nodded. Not sure why I was disappointed that it hadn't been Harvey, but I was.

He asked me a few more questions and then said that a detective would probably be in touch with me the next day. I stared at the phone. I needed to call Randolph, but it was after three in the morning there. It would have to wait until tomorrow afternoon.

I returned to the kitchen, where the conversation immediately died as I stepped into the room. I inhaled and then released it slowly.

"I'm only going to ask this once; was anyone in here aware that he was doing that?"

Everyone answered no immediately as they shook their heads. "That's messed up, Chef," Malick said.

Tobias, who had taken over Ricardo's position, frowned. "I can't believe he did that to you because he wanted your job. I'm glad you smacked him. If you hadn't, I would have slugged him."

"Yeah, that wasn't right," Ben called out. " I can't believe he hurt people to make you look bad."

A few others voiced their thoughts, and I felt a little better knowing that they all disapproved of what he had done.

The meals were done, and we were starting our cleanup for the night when there was another bang at the back door, and I sighed. "Good god! What now?" I muttered and then raised my voice. "David, will you get that?" I called over my shoulder as I prepared to break my station down.

"Got it, Chef!" He opened the door, and I expected police to come rushing through again, but no one did. Instead, Dave stood at the back door for a moment, talking to someone. He glanced toward me, grinned, and then spoke to someone before he took something from them and closed the door.

I didn't see what was in his hand, and he held it behind his back until he reached me. "Chef, you have a delivery," he said as he attempted to hide a smile as he held an envelope out.

It looked strangely familiar, and as I took it, my heart fluttered nervously. I pulled the card out, and the original words that were written were scratched out with new ones written under it. "May I have this dance, Ali Davidson?"

My eyes snapped to the back door, and before I even consciously knew what to do, I was moving toward the door, shrugging out of my chef's coat as I went.

I threw open the door, expecting to see Harvey standing there, but instead, there was no one. Well, no one that I could see right away. What I did see was a large spotlight pointing at the center of the alley.

CHAPTER TWENTY-NINE

HARVEY

*A*s much as I wanted to hurry things, I didn't dare. If everything went as I hoped, I'd have a lifetime to be with Ali, and two days wouldn't matter much.

I was preparing to head over to Mike's when I got a call from him. I hit the speaker. "I was just getting ready to head over."

"Yeah, well, I think Ali might have something big to celebrate tonight."

"What's that?"

"Trevor and I were watching the video in the kitchen tonight, and Trevor noticed one of the guys go into the locker room, then come out, and he was wearing a glove. He approached his station, touched the food, then slipped the glove off and into a baggie before he deposited it into the trash."

"What was with the glove?"

"I can't say for sure, but I'm pretty sure he probably had some type of container in his things that held the E. coli bacteria in the locker room, and put it on his gloved hand, touched it to the food, and bam, contaminated it."

"What are you going to do about it?"

"We already did. As soon as we saw it, we called the police

and EMS and told them what was going on. They took him into custody, and he admitted he was doing it to get Ali fired so he could have the Head Chef position."

"Are you kidding me? He was after her job, and that was worth almost killing people?"

"Yeah, I guess," Mike said. "So, Ali's probably ready to celebrate."

"Then I guess this is good timing." I paused. "That is if she accepts my invitation."

"She will. I have no doubt. The only problem is going to be that it is raining."

"I don't care about a little rain."

"You sure you don't want to do it another night?"

"No, I'm ready." I chuckled. "Actually, the first time I ran into Ali, it was in a rainstorm."

"Really?"

I proceeded to tell him about it quickly, and then told him I was heading down to the restaurant.

He told me he'd meet me there, and we disconnected the call. I was nervous about what I was going to do, but Ali had told me to come to her. She had told me to ask her to dance, so that is what I was going to do. I owed her this plus a huge apology.

When I arrived at the restaurant, I parked out front on the street and walked down the alley. Mike was parked back there, and he was setting up some speakers and the spotlights that he had brought under a little tent. We were going to start with one light, and then he would turn on two more to brighten the entire area so we could see in the alley. It wasn't a spiffy hotel ballroom, but I hoped that she would appreciate the gesture.

The rain was coming down lightly, and I hoped that it didn't stop her from taking me up on my offer. I had a feeling that it wouldn't, but I could be wrong. I sure had been wrong about things before.

Mike knocked on the back door to the restaurant, and a younger guy opened it. He wore a t-shirt and messy apron around his waist. I could just make out what Mike was telling him.

"We need you to do us a favor. Can you give this to Ali Davidson?"

"What's this about?" he asked as I stepped out of the shadows. The kid grinned. "Oh, man! Yeah, I'll give it to her."

"Thanks." The kid turned and disappeared into the restaurant again. Mike dashed off to the side where his car was parked, and I stepped back into the shadows again. Last night in the middle of the night, I had come here and walked the dance, making sure we would have the room and that it wouldn't be a safety issue. It was perfect.

It was a minute before the door flew open, and Ali stood there. Her chef's coat in one hand, the invite in the other, as she searched the darkness. When she noticed the spotlight, a smile began to slip over her face.

"Ali Davidson, I owe you an apology," I called out from the other side of the alley.

"Do you, Harvey Melton?"

"Yes, I do. I jumped to a conclusion. I should have asked. I'm sorry."

"How are you going to make it up to me?"

"May I have this dance and show you?"

I saw some of her coworkers peeking around her into the darkness. Ali stepped forward, and someone leaned against the door to hold it open.

"Here?"

"Yes, here."

She looked up at the rain and laughed. "Why not!"

"Music, Mike."

A moment later, the music started, and Ali was grinning as she pushed her chef's coat into someone's hands and began to walk toward me. We met in the spotlight just like we had on the ballroom floor, and this time, when she lifted my chin, I knew that I had won as I stared into her eyes.

As Ali twirled away from me, Mike hit the switch, and the alley lit up. I noticed briefly that there were several people off to the side, watching us, but I didn't care. I wanted everyone to see us. I wanted everyone to know.

Ali and I danced even better than we originally had. It didn't matter that we weren't on a fancy floor or that it was raining. Our bodies fit against each other, and there was a stronger connection now than there had been that night.

By the time we were done with the dance, we were breathing hard and soaked, but we stared at one another as I cupped her cheek. "I'm so sorry, Ali. I was a bastard for how I treated you."

"I forgive you. I know you didn't know. I figured that out. You thought I was cheating on Blake."

"I've had it done to me; I couldn't do it to someone else. My conscience just stabbed me in my gut that night. As much as I wanted you, I couldn't because I didn't think you were free."

She ran her fingers over my cheek, blinking back the raindrops as they fell against her lashes. "I'm sorry that I didn't tell you. I should have."

"When you were in the kitchen, later that day, I heard what you said. I did feel it. I do feel it. I feel so much when I am with you, Ali. I think that day that we first ran into each other in the storm, well, I think I felt it then too, but I was distracted."

"I think I did too, Harvey."

I leaned my forehead to hers. "Ali, I want to get to know you better. I want to learn everything about you and fall in love with you, build a future. It just feels right."

She wrapped her arms around my neck. "I'm pretty sure I agree with you, but there is one thing that I need to know before I commit to anything."

I leaned back and frowned. "Okay, what? Anything."

"During the show, you said you wanted to be able to cook for your woman."

"Yes, I enjoy cooking."

She nibbled on her bottom lip. "Do you use jar sauce? Because if you do, that's a deal breaker."

I threw my head back and laughed. "I have been known to use it on occasion, but I make a mean alfredo sauce from scratch."

"Scratch, huh?"

I grinned at her as I took her face in my hands. "I'm going to kiss you now, Ali."

"Hurry up, Harvey."

I didn't waste any more time as I brought our lips together. Neither of us knew for sure if our relationship would last, but for the first time in my life, I honestly wanted to do anything I could to make it happen.

There was something about Ali that spoke to my very soul, and I hoped that she felt it too. As we stood in the rain and kissed, there were claps and whistles off to the side. All but one light was turned off so that we stood in the middle of the single spotlight.

"Harvey, will you be my partner, now and forever, however long this lasts for us?"

"Yes, I will, Ali, but I have a feeling that it's going to be a very long time. No matter what storm comes our way, I think we'll be able to make it through."

She leaned forward, her eyes sparkling, her lips almost touching mine. "Just ask me to dance, Mr. Sexy, and we can let our bodies do the talking."

THE END

I hope you enjoyed Unexpected Storms, if you did, please consider leaving a brief review. It's the best way to tell an author you enjoyed their book!

If you haven't already, make sure to check out the rest of the Unexpected Series.

Unexpected Packages, Book 1

Lexi Miller restarted her life five years ago and has been living a regimented routine ever since. With a great job and a best friend who tries everything to get her to break-out of her boring life, it's not until her birthday present arrives at her door, opened by a stranger, that things finally start to get interesting.

Alex Miller is ready for his second career after retiring from the military. He's excited to start training contractors in safety issues and getting to know his daughter after being away for so many years.

When a package addressed to him shows up on his doorstep,

he is kind enough to deliver the box to the rightful owner. When Lexi opens the door, Alex quickly realizes that he's found the beautiful woman he has been catching peeks of as she comes and goes from the building.

From misunderstandings to new beginnings, Alex and Lexi come together, but a business trip threatens their future right before Valentine's Day, and neither is sure they will ever be reunited.

Unexpected Arrivals, Book 2

Trevor Vaughn loves his job, his women, and his bachelor lifestyle. Sadly, for him, all of that might change when Davina Daniels walks into his office pushing a stroller.

The problem is that Trevor doesn't have any idea who Davina is. After she explains that he is the baby's father, he finds himself clueless as to what to do next.

After begging for her help, Davina and Trevor begin to form a friendship that will bring them together in time for their friend's wedding and a single night of steamy romance.

It's after their moments of bliss when words are misspoken, strangers show up, and baby Devon is raced to the hospital that their newfound romance is put to the test. Will Trevor and Davina find a way back to each other, or will the storms continue to crash down over them?

Unexpected Trouble, Book 3

Big things are happening at Safety Zone Security, and before a client meeting, Gregory Blaire heads down to Cocoa's Coffee Café to grab some much-needed caffeine. Running into his high school sweetheart was almost the last thing he excepted, but the jewelry store heist that went wrong tops even that.

As hard as Maggie Valor works to build her career as a

serious journalist, she's stuck as a romance advice columnist, and she'll do just about anything to change that. When Maggie runs into Greg and then gets taken hostage, her mind is torn between the story and the man who broke her heart.

With Maggie putting herself in the way of danger, stepping into Safety Zone Security to help with a client, and then pushing to join an operation, all Greg can see is trouble. Now the police are questioning her, a thief is out to get her, and the only thing Greg can do is take her on a delivery operation to keep her out of more unexpected trouble.

Unexpected Storms, Book 4

Ali Davidson is ready for a serious relationship; only the conventional methods aren't much help in finding the right man for her. Could being a contestant on the May I Have This Dance television show help her find love on the dance floor? Her friend and producer, Holly Melton, believes it will be the perfect way to find a connection.

Harvey Melton works long hours and travels a lot, but while burning time off from work, his sister begs for his help. Harvey would do anything for his sister, including dance on her silly television show.

Ali has to decide between her three dance partners, which two she will ask back for a second dance, and then choose between them to explore a relationship. With Ali trying to make her decision between the two final men, she has significant distractions in her kitchen.

When more patrons get sick, and the threat of the restaurant and her reputation are on the line, Holly steps in to get Ali help and enlists the guys at Safety Zone Security. When they show up, Ali is surprised to see Harvey, and the attraction between these two is undeniable and stormy.

Coming Soon:
Unexpected Desires
Unexpected Ties

ABOUT THE AUTHOR

Stacy Eaton is a USA Today Best Selling author and began her writing career in October of 2010. Stacy took an early retirement from law enforcement after over fifteen years of service in 2016, with her last three years in investigations and crime scene investigation to write full time.

Stacy resides in southeastern Pennsylvania with her husband, who works in law enforcement, and her teen daughter. She also has a son who is currently serving in the United States Navy and has two grandchildren.

Be sure to visit www.stacyeaton.com for updates and more information on her books.

Sign up for all the latest information on Stacy's Newsletter!

ALSO BY STACY EATON

Paranormal Romance:

My Blood Runs Blue Series

My Blood Runs Blue, Book 1 **

The Pulse of Blue Blood, Book 2 (Short Story) **

Blue Blood for Life, Book 3 **

Mixing the Blue Blood, Book 4 ***

Blue Bloods Final Destiny, Book 5 ***

The Return of Blue Blood Series:

Kristin: Blue Blood Returns, Book 1

Hugh: Blue Blood Compelled, Book 2

Zander: Blue Blood Reborn, Book 3

Lena: Blue Blood Desired, Book 4 (coming soon)

Garda ~ Welcome to the Realm

Domestic Violence – Crime - Suspense:

Whether I'll Live or Die**

Barbara's Plea

You're Not Alone**

Romantic Suspense:

Liveon ~ No Evil ***

Second Shield ***

Distorted Loyalty**

Six Days of Memories **

Second Shield II: The Return ***

Contemporary Romance:
Tempt Me Too**
Finding the Strength

Finding Love in Special Places:
Stacy's Short Story Series
Finding Love on Christmas Vacation
Finding Love on the Summer Surf
Finding Love with Dear Santa
Finding Love with a Champagne Toast

Heart of the Family Series
Mistletoe & Cocoa Kisses, Book 1 **
Roses & Champagne Kisses, Book 2 **
Orchids & Hurricane Kisses, Book 3 **
Carnations & Hot Toddy Kisses, Book 4 **

Heal Me Series
Cured, Book 1 **
Revived, Book 2
Mended, Book 3
Rescued, Book 4

The Celebration Series
Tangled in Tinsel, Book 1 **
Tears to Cheers, Book 2 **
Heathens to Hearts, Book 3 **
Rainbows Bring Riches, Book 4 ***

Sweet as Sugar, Book 5 ***

Making Mom Mad, Book 6 ***

Sparklers or Spankings, Book 7 ***

Raffles to Rattles, Book 8 ***

Flirting with Fireworks, Book 9 ***

Working under Wheels, Book 10 ***

Masquerading at Midnight, Book 11 ***

Blessings & Beans, Book 12 ***

Velvet & Vows, Book 13 ***

The Celebration Series Box Sets:

Part One: Books 1-5

Part Two: Books 6-9

Part Three: Books 10-13

The Sometimes Series:

Sometimes You Win, Book 1**

Sometimes You Lose, Book 2**

Sometimes You Play The Game, Book 3**

The Sometimes Series: Win, Lose & Play Set **

Pleasure Your Fantasies Series

Mistletoe Fantasies, Book 1 **

Whispered Fantasies, Book 2

Secret Fantasies, Book 3

The Twisted Love Series

with Amy Manemann Co-Author

Love Lorn, Book 1 (Manemann)**

Love Torn, Book 2 (Eaton)**

Love Inked, Book 3

Love Drowned, Book 4

Love Carved, Book 5

Love Trapped, Book 6

Love Crossed, Book 7

Love Twisted, Book 8

Love Lies, Book 9

Rise Again Warrior Series

Mission: Believe, Book 1 **

Mission: Accept, Book 2 **

Mission: Repair, (coming soon)

Loving a Young Series

Wesley, Book 1

Henley, Book 2

The Unexpected Series

Unexpected Packages

Unexpected Arrivals

Unexpected Trouble

Unexpected Storms

Unexpected Desires (coming soon)

Unexpected Ties (coming soon)

** These books are also available on Audio

*** These books are coming to Audio soon

List Update 10-14-20

www.ingramcontent.com/pod-product-compliance
Lightning Source LLC
Chambersburg PA
CBHW031426200626
46814CB00016B/2331